**'Alex…I wa**

I like hearing th
watching the w
with you. Intellectually and emotionally we re
a perfect match.'

'I'll end up hurting you, Jordanne,' he confessed, his tone laced with desire and regret.

'What if you don't hurt me? What if we fall in love and end up living happily ever after?' she pressed gently, hoping she didn't scare him off.

'You're deluding yourself,' he said softly as he gazed deeply into her eyes. 'Jordanne.' He slowly shook his head. 'I'm a selfish man. If I don't hold you in my arms tonight, if I don't kiss you the way I've been dreaming about for the past month, if I pass up this opportunity… I'll regret it.'

'Then don't pass it up.'

'I'm sorry, Jordanne,' he whispered, before his lips claimed hers in an electrifying kiss.

**Lucy Clark** began writing romance in her early teens and immediately knew she'd found her 'calling' in life. After working as a secretary in a busy teaching hospital, she turned her hand to writing medical romance. She currently lives in Adelaide, Australia, and has the desire to travel the world with her husband. Lucy largely credits her writing success to the support of her husband, family and friends.

**Recent titles by the same author:**

THE CONSULTANT'S CONFLICT
A SURGEON'S REPUTATION
PARTNERS FOR EVER

# THE SURGEON'S SECRET

BY
LUCY CLARK

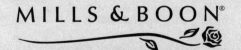

MILLS & BOON®

To Murph—Thanks for all of your help.
Hope you like Sky. Love, Brades.
Romans 10:10

*First published in Great Britain 2001*
*Harlequin Mills & Boon Limited,*
*Eton House, 18-24 Paradise Road, Richmond, Surrey TW9 1SR*

© Lucy Clark 2001

ISBN 0 263 82694 5

*Set in Times Roman 10½ on 11¾ pt.*
*03-1001-48499*

*Printed and bound in Spain*
*by Litografia Rosés, S.A., Barcelona*

# CHAPTER ONE

'WE'VE been working together for three weeks,' Jordanne McElroy complained down the telephone receiver to her good friend Kirsten Doyle. The two women had known each other since med school. '*Three weeks*,' Jordanne stressed. 'And *still* all I get from him are monosyllables.'

Kirsten laughed. 'Surely it's not *all* monosyllables.'

'Well, except when we're discussing patients,' Jordanne acknowledged. 'Otherwise monosyllables.'

'Jordanne, you have to settle down. Alex is probably just…overwhelmed by you.'

'Overwhelmed? Why?' Jordanne frowned. She drummed her fingers on her desk, waiting impatiently for Kirsten's answer.

'Jordanne, the first time you met the man you threw your arms around him and kissed him.'

'I *didn't* kiss him,' Jordanne corrected immediately. 'I *hugged* him, yes, but he'd just saved Joel's life. Wouldn't you thank someone who'd saved *your* brother's life?' Jordanne demanded.

'Of course I would. All I meant was that Alex probably would have preferred a handshake.'

'I won't change who I am,' Jordanne warned, and then sighed, realising she was probably overreacting. 'I can't help it if I come across as a little…exuberant sometimes.' She shrugged even though Kirsten couldn't see her.

'Sometimes?'

'Oh, all right—*most* of the time. But it's one of my better

5

qualities. It's who I am. Alex will just have to learn to accept it.'

'You both need to find common ground soon otherwise the research project might suffer.'

'I wouldn't let it suffer,' Jordanne stated stubbornly. 'Alex Page may be head of the orthopaedic department at Canberra General Hospital, and I may be employed as his research fellow for the next twelve months but even if he doesn't say another word to me for the rest of my contract there's no way in the world that I would *ever* let the work suffer. Especially when he's gone to so much trouble to obtain funding for my position. We're both professionals.'

'That's what I love about you,' Kirsten stated strongly. 'Your bold determination never wanes, regardless of what challenges you're facing.'

'I just can't believe how…blunt the man is,' Jordanne said, not pacified by her friend's praise. 'In my family, we were always taught that manners meant everything and cost nothing. Alex Page has the manners of a bad-tempered go-rilla. Quite frankly, Kirsten, I'm surprised that he and Jed have remained friends for so long.'

'Men obviously look for different types of friendships to women.'

'No. That's not it. Not in this instance at any rate. Jed is my oldest brother. All of us—all *six* of us—were raised knowing the importance of good manners.' Jordanne looked at the Monet print that hung on her office wall opposite her desk. She'd positioned it there to help her relax— it wasn't working. The only other wall hanging she had was a painting her sister Jasmine had done a few years ago.

'I've not had one please or thank you from him since I started. He may be tall, dark and handsome and have half of the females in this hospital swooning at his feet, but not

me. I have little time and no patience with people like him.'
Even as Jordanne said the words out loud, she knew they
didn't ring true. Her thoughts had turned to Alex Page far
too often for her liking during the past three weeks and that
implied she had a *lot* of time for 'people like him'.

'Who are you trying to kid? You've got your knickers
in a twist over him.' Kirsten was silent for a second before
saying, 'He *is* rather good-looking but, then, we all know
I'm a sucker for a tall man with dark brown hair and blue
eyes.'

'I thought you didn't fancy him?' Jordanne said, ignoring
the hint of irritation she'd experienced at her friend's
words.

'I don't, well, at least, he doesn't *do* anything for me.
I've only met him once, remember, and even then Sally
and Jed were around. Just a minute,' Kirsten said, and
Jordanne heard someone talking to her friend. 'I've got to
go, Jordanne. My first patient has arrived.'

No sooner were the words out of Kirsten's mouth than
Jordanne's office door burst opened and there stood the
man she was talking about, his hand still on the doorhandle.

Alex's gaze met hers before his eyes dipped to look at
her clothes. His gaze settled briefly on the gold fob chain
that rested on top of her royal blue silk blouse near the
valley of her breasts. Jordanne felt tingles flood throughout
her entire body at the caress from his gaze. Her breath
caught in her throat as she waited for him to speak.

His gaze finally met hers once more. 'Clinic.' The word
was gruff before he closed the door behind him.

Jordanne breathed out slowly, amazed at the way he
made her feel. 'Oh, he's good,' she told Kirsten who was
still on the other end of the phone. 'He just opened my
door, made me feel as though I was on fire with one simple

look and then *poof*, he's gone like a magician, but not before he delivers his monosyllabic order.'

'From what you've just said, it sounds as though he's attracted to you,' Kirsten ventured. 'Why don't you try touching him—accidentally on purpose, mind you—in clinic. Just brush your arm up against his and watch his reaction.'

'Kirsten.' Jordanne shook her head even though her friend couldn't see. 'You're just jumping to conclusions. I'm nothing more than a lackey to him.'

'Even so—try it. Call me tonight and let me know how it goes. Right now we both have Monday morning to get through.'

Jordanne said goodbye and ended the call, still feeling irritated with her new boss for making her so confused. Forcing herself to do some deep breathing, she crossed over to her white coat that hung by the door and put it on. Reaching for her stethoscope which she'd left on her desk, she looped it around the back of her neck, making sure her long brown hair was still secure in the bun she'd wound it into that morning, before opening the door.

Jordanne hadn't *wanted* to be attracted to Alex Page, but she was. She'd been instantly aware of his magnificent physique that very first time she'd hugged him. The revelation had surprised and delighted her, but ever since she'd started working with him the physical attraction she'd felt had been nudged aside in light of his manners.

Things just didn't add up. When her brother, Jed, had initially told her about this job, he'd prophesied that she'd like working with his good friend. Sally, Jordanne's friend since med school and now her sister-in-law-to-be, had also thought Jordanne and Alex would work well together.

Two people—whose opinions she'd not only listened to but trusted—were turning out to be wrong. *Very* wrong.

'Something's not right,' she mumbled to herself as she walked into the orthopaedic outpatient department that was swarming with patients. Although she might be annoyed and irritated with her new boss, she was also mildly intrigued to know *why* he was so blunt with her.

'Hi, Jordanne,' Sister Trudy Elliot greeted her as she entered the consulting area. 'How's that sexy brother of yours progressing?'

Jordanne smiled, glad to have something other than Alex Page to focus on. 'Which one?' Jordanne teased. 'I have four brothers, remember.'

'Joel, of course.' Trudy laughed. 'I definitely wouldn't mean Jed, otherwise Sally would have my head.'

'Oh? So you know?' Jordanne looked puzzled. As far as she knew, neither Sally nor Jed had set foot inside the hospital since their return from Sydney yesterday evening, and *she* hadn't said anything. Jed had only proposed to Sally last Friday night—in front of the entire McElroy clan. It had been so romantic and it had been obvious to everyone who'd witnessed the event that they'd only had eyes for each other. Jordanne was so happy for both of them and silently wished that she, too, would find happiness in love—sooner rather than later.

'Know what?' Trudy asked, her interest piqued.

'Uh…' she stalled, realising her error, instantly mad at Alex Page. It was all his fault. If her mind hadn't been so preoccupied with him she wouldn't have made that slip. 'That Joel's now in Sydney,' she said, hopefully covering up her mistake.

'Yes.' Trudy frowned at her. 'I know Alex discharged him home and handed his case over to another orthopod in Sydney. That's why I'm asking.'

'Well, he was doing fine when I left my parents' house

yesterday. Mum's a real nurturer so Joel will receive the best care at home.'

'It must be nice to come from such a loving family.' Trudy sighed.

'Patients,' a deep male voice boomed, and Jordanne turned from Trudy to see Alex walking towards her, hospital case notes cradled in his arm. He stopped and dished out two files to Jordanne before nodding and walking away.

Jordanne looked to Trudy but the nurse obviously didn't seem to think there was anything wrong as she checked her watch.

'Goodness, Alex is right. We'd better get this clinic under way or we'll all be running late for the rest of the day.'

Jordanne entered her consulting room and ground her teeth together in exasperation. She only had a few minutes to settle in at her desk before Trudy showed the first patient in and the clinic began.

Jordanne saw one patient after the other, and just before midday the phone on her desk shrilled to life.

'Dr McElroy,' she answered absent-mindedly as she finished writing up some case notes.

'Have you got a moment?' Alex's deep voice caught her off guard.

'Uh, yes. Problem?'

'Just an interesting case I thought you might like to look at.'

'Which consulting room are you in?'

'Three.'

'I'll be right there,' Jordanne replied. She finished writing up her notes and stood, placing the completed file on the desk for the clerks to deal with. She walked across the corridor, tapped briefly on the door to consulting room three and walked in. It wasn't the first time Alex had asked her to take a look at either a patient or X-rays. A lot of the doctors sought each other's opinions, but still she felt a little flurry of excitement zip through her at Alex asking for *her* opinion.

'Take a look at these.' Alex pointed to some radiographs up on the viewing machine. He was standing beside it, taking another look, as though he didn't believe what he was seeing. 'The patient presented at A and E about half an hour ago.'

Jordanne did as he suggested. As she looked at the films, she became aware of Alex's body very close to hers. The scent of his cologne teased her senses and Jordanne forced herself not to like it. She could also feel the warmth radiating from him at their close proximity and tried to take a step back, only to encounter the edge of the desk. She thought about what Kirsten had suggested and wondered if she was game enough to try it. She moved in again and took another look at the X-rays—*really* concentrating on them this time.

The patient in question had fractured his tibia on three separate occasions and each time it had fractured in exactly the same place and in exactly the same way.

Jordanne looked at the dates on the X-rays. The dates were the same on each occasion, only the years had changed. 'Exactly two years apart on the first two and now one year since the last break.' She shook her head in bemused amazement and looked at Alex. 'What are the odds?' she asked rhetorically.

'I thought he might be an interesting case for the research study.'

'I take it he's not a professional athlete,' Jordanne stated. 'If he is, he's in big trouble with such an alarming rate of injury.'

'No. Once a year, he plays a rugby reunion match with his old college mates. They always play the match on the fourth of September because that's the date they won their college grand final.'

Jordanne checked her watch and looked at Alex with a frown. 'But it's not even lunchtime. What time do they start?'

'Usually around ten o'clock, and once the game is over they spend the rest of the day at the pub, catching up and enjoying themselves.' He changed the X-ray to display another view.

'Sounds like a wild bunch.' Jordanne shook her head in bemusement. 'And each year…' she peered at the name on the X-rays '…Mr Dylan Foster sustains a fissured fracture to his tibia.'

'Yes,' Alex responded.

'Amazing! What about the year he *didn't* fracture his tibia?'

'He was sick with shingles.' Although Alex said the words matter-of-factly, Jordanne turned her head sharply to gaze at him. She watched as the corners of his mouth twitched into a small smile.

'Oh, the poor man.' Jordanne laughed, feeling sorry for the patient.

'What's so funny?' Ian Parks, Alex's senior registrar, asked as he came into the room.

'Dylan Foster has returned,' Alex informed him.

'Of course, it's the fourth of September.' Ian walked over to the viewing box. He stood next to Jordanne and peered at the films.

'I presume he fractured it in the same way?' Ian asked, looking at Alex. The two men's gazes met over Jordanne's head.

'Exactly,' Alex replied.

Jordanne frowned, feeling slightly left out. She waved her hand between them. 'Hello! I'm still here. I may only be five foot, five tall, but, please, don't talk over my head. My brothers have done it to me for years and let me tell you right now—I don't particularly like it.' She smiled to belie the severity of her words.

Ian Parks laughed. 'You poor thing. What's the weather like down there?'

'Stop it,' she replied with a chuckle. 'Just because you're both over six foot there's no need to rub it in.'

'I'm exactly six foot,' Ian told her. 'Alex is a few inches taller than me. How tall are you, boss? Six-three or six-four?'

Alex looked from Ian to Jordanne, his gaze remaining on her for a fraction longer.

Jordanne allowed her gaze to start at his shoes, working her way up to his dark, immaculately groomed hair. It was a quick perusal but one that left her wishing she could have taken more time. 'I'd guess you'd be about six foot four—same as Jed,' Jordanne surmised before he could answer.

He swallowed before nodding. 'Yes.' He looked purposely back to the X-rays.

'Are you going to include Dylan in your study?' Ian asked Jordanne.

'*My* study,' Alex corrected his registrar.

'*Our* study,' Jordanne said, and reached out to pull one of the radiographs from the viewer. As she did so, her arm brushed against Alex's firm torso. Her breath caught in her throat and a rush of wildfire spread throughout her body, warming her instantly. Jordanne dropped her hand to her side, the film forgotten.

'Right,' he agreed with a nod. Again, their gazes held for a brief moment and Jordanne felt her knees weaken. Alex *was* a devastatingly attractive man. His blue eyes were as dark as the sea in a storm and they were looking at her with surprise. Had *he* felt the awareness she'd just experienced? Not possible, she rationalised. Not if his attitude during the past few weeks was any indication.

She thought back to what she and Kirsten had discussed only a few hours ago. She hadn't *meant* to brush up against Alex, even though she'd thought about it when she'd walked into the room. She tried to remember his reaction so she and Kirsten could discuss it later.

Jordanne turned her attention to Ian. 'Probably,' she finally said, realising Ian's question still required an answer. 'Would it be possible to have further scanning and tests done?'

'The second time he presented, that's exactly what we did,' Ian informed her. 'Are these the case notes, Alex?' he asked, pointing to an open file on Alex's consulting desk.

'Yes.' Alex handed them to Ian who took a quick look before offering them to Jordanne.

'Is he still here?' She accepted the case notes and flicked through them, scanning the previous outpatient notes.

'He's in the plaster room, getting a cast on his leg. I want him in overnight for observation,' Alex said.

'That will mean all his drunk rugby buddies will be around to see him later today,' Ian added. 'I'd better notify the ward sister or she won't be too happy.'

'Good idea.' Alex nodded.

Jordanne gave Dylan Foster's case notes to Ian so he could make the necessary arrangements.

'I'll get onto it right away.' Ian walked out of the room, leaving Jordanne and Alex alone.

'A very…unique case,' Jordanne remarked after a moment's silence. 'Mr Foster will fit nicely into the amateur athlete section of the study.'

'Agreed.' Alex leaned back against the desk, his arms

folded across his chest. Still he didn't venture to say anything.

Back to monosyllables, she thought. 'I presume a case study has already been done on Mr Foster?' Jordanne asked, trying not to be intimidated by his stance.

'Yes.'

She clenched her jaw tightly together as Alex began to annoy her once more. 'Do you think I could do an updated presentation for the grand round next week?'

'No.'

'Why not?' Jordanne was now having trouble controlling her rising temper. 'He's an incredible case. I've never seen anything like it before and there are quite a few new staff members who won't be familiar with the previous findings. Isn't that what the grand round is for? I mean, everybody who's anybody is at that meeting for the purpose of learning about new and interesting cases.' There, she thought. Try and answer *that* with a monosyllable.

He gave her a thoughtful look before nodding. 'You'll be too busy. I'll get Ian to do it. He did the last one.'

Jordanne grinned exuberantly. She'd managed to get him to say more than one word in that answer.

'Something funny?' Alex asked, frowning—a look she was positive he'd been born with, he did it so often to her.

Jordanne instantly wiped the smile from her face. 'No.' The one-word reply was her crowning glory. Her lips might not be smiling but her eyes were twinkling with delight. When her stomach grumbled its protest at the lack of food, the humour died altogether. She glanced up at Alex, not sure whether or not he'd heard. His raised eyebrow indicated he had.

For a brief second the world appeared to stand still. There was silent communication going on between them— a communication that both were trying hard to ignore. His gaze displayed an emotion Jordanne hadn't witnessed before and briefly—so quickly, she thought she'd imagined it—his gaze dipped to her lips.

Her stomach fluttered in anticipation and her breathing increased. Her lips parted to let the air out and the tip of her tongue slipped between them, moistening their suddenly dry state.

Alex cleared his throat. 'So, do you want to see him?'

'Who?' Jordanne's mind was a complete blank. 'Oh, Dylan Foster. You said he was in the plaster room, didn't you?'

'Yes.' Alex turned on his heel and walked out of the consulting room. Jordanne followed behind. The plaster room was only two doors down. Alex knocked before entering and held the door for Jordanne.

'Thank you,' she said, a little surprised he'd actually waited.

'Mr Foster.' Alex addressed the man lying on the examination couch. The plaster orderly was almost finished. 'This is Dr McElroy, my associate.'

'Well, hello, there.' Dylan Foster leered at Jordanne. 'Where have you been hiding all my life?'

Jordanne forced a smile and ignored his question. 'Mr Foster—' she began.

'My friends call me Dylan,' he corrected in what she could only presume was his attempt at a sexy voice. 'You can, too.'

'Thank you so much,' Jordanne answered. 'Dr Page has brought your unique case to my attention. I'm currently involved in a study of lower limb fractures and a new medication which helps repair fractures more quickly. It's a non-steroidal, non-performance-enhancing medication. In the study, we're mainly focusing on professionally trained athletes, but we'll also be including case studies of amateur and non-athletes. As you periodically play rugby and have sustained injuries from it, you're *perfect*—' Jordanne smiled sweetly as she said the word '—for our study.'

'Am I, now?' He raised one eyebrow at her suggestively.

'If you're interested, I'd be more than happy to supply you with further information. It's important that the participants of the study understand exactly what's involved.'

'Well, how about you and me get together tonight and discuss things in more detail?'

'I have some meetings this afternoon but I can certainly come to the ward to discuss the study.'

'It's a date,' he said, and as he lowered his eyelids in what Jordanne could only surmise was supposed to be his 'sexy' look, she was hard-pressed to keep from laughing out loud.

'I'll see you then.' With that, she turned and walked out, fearing she wouldn't be able to control her mirth for much longer.

Alex was hard on her heels. He gently placed his hand beneath her elbow and propelled her into his consulting room. He closed the door behind them. Jordanne tried hard to ignore the tingling throughout her body which his touch had evoked and instead glared down at his hand on her arm, indicating she wasn't too impressed with his urging. He removed his hand instantly.

'What on earth were you playing at in there?' he demanded briskly.

'Sorry?' Jordanne frowned. 'I don't follow.'

'You were flirting with a patient.'

'What? Have you lost your mind? I was *not* flirting with a patient,' she denied instantly. '*He* was flirting with *me*. There's a *big* difference.'

'Oh, please. You did everything to encourage him. He's

not that important to the study. We can find another patient to participate.'

'He's not a threat, Alex. I've handled worse than him before. Women learn these survival skills to protect themselves from leering males in high school. It's the quiet, shy men that are a lot more dangerous than the likes of Mr Dylan Foster.' She looked at him pointedly, indicating she meant men like him. 'Dylan's all bluster. Trust me, Alex. Growing up with four brothers has taught me a thing or two about men.'

'You have no idea what you're talking about.'

Jordanne saw red. 'How can you say that? You hardly know me.' She took a deep breath, knowing that she had to cool it.

Alex shoved his hands into his trouser pockets and frowned.

'Look,' Jordanne began again, more calmly. 'I'll be talking to him in the ward. There'll be plenty of staff around. It's not as though we're going to have a candlelit dinner in the privacy of his home. It will still be daylight outside.'

'Let me know when you're going to see him,' Alex insisted.

'Fine.' Her tone was clipped. 'Come along if that's what makes you happy but, remember, you did *employ* me to do this research study. If you're going to be looking over my shoulder every five minutes, second-guessing what's going on, I might as well go back to Sydney right now. My job was to lighten your load and get this project up and running. Now, you either trust me to do it or I leave. It's as simple as that.' Jordanne turned to walk out of his room and Alex quickly closed the distance between them. He placed a hand on her shoulder and turned her around to face him, dropping his hand almost the instant he'd made contact.

'I'm very protective of my staff.' Alex focused on her lips for an instant before meeting her gaze again. 'If Mr Foster continues with his present attitude, it could be bordering on sexual harassment and I don't want *any* staff in my department to have to endure it. Not from other staff members and not from patients. I won't stand for it and neither will the hospital. Besides, Jed would have my head if he thought I'd let anything happen to you.'

Jordanne looked up at him, knowing she could quite easily drown in those gorgeous blue eyes. 'I appreciate your concern, Alex, but I'm a big girl,' she told him, amazed at how gooey inside his words had made her feel. *He cared*— he *really* cared. 'I know the hospital's policy regarding sexual harassment. If I have any problems with Dylan Foster— groping hands, that sort of thing—I'll report it immediately and you can take over his involvement in the study. But to tell you the truth, I think Mr Foster is all talk and no action. What's the bet he's married with a couple of kids but just has to look heroic in front of any other man?' she suggested, hoping to lighten the atmosphere a bit.

In the past fifteen minutes she'd seen more of the *real* Alex Page than she had during the entire time she'd been working with him.

Alex considered what she'd said. 'All right,' he conceded. 'Go and see him by yourself but if—'

'I promise, Alex,' she told him seriously. Her stomach growled again and Jordanne rolled her eyes, glad that something had broken the sombre mood. 'I think I'd better go finish up with my patients before my stomach protests any louder.'

This time when she went to open the door he didn't stop her. Jordanne returned to her own consulting room, even more puzzled than when she'd first begun the clinic. Alex had shown such genuine concern for her that perhaps, just perhaps, during their time of working together he'd been covering up other feelings he hadn't wanted Jordanne to know about.

She considered herself quite experienced at reading the signals a man could send a woman he liked. Now she was certain that that was *exactly* what Alex Page had been do-ing.

'Wait until I tell Kirsten,' she whispered to herself before a knock on the door brought her back to reality. Her next patient was shown in but nothing could shift Jordanne's good mood.

She and Kirsten discussed Alex—his every word and ac-tion—at length and in detail for the rest of the week. He had still remained a little standoffish with her and had asked for a complete report on her meeting with Dylan Foster. Jordanne had been pleased to tell him that Mr Foster was indeed married and his wife had been present when she'd spoken with him.

'It sounds as though Alex wants to keep his distance from you,' Kirsten said thoughtfully as Jordanne poured her another cup of coffee.

'Oh, and there's another thing,' Jordanne added. 'I was talking to Sally yesterday and she asked me about my din-ner with Alex. I told her I hadn't been out to dinner with him.'

'Of course.' Kirsten raised her free hand to her head. 'Why didn't I remember that sooner? Alex's dinner.'

'You know about this?' Jordanne asked with surprise.

'That he takes all his new surgical staff out to dinner? Yes. You know I went out with Alex, Sally and Jed—that was supposed to be Sally's business dinner with Alex.'

'Oh?' Jordanne frowned. 'I didn't know that.'

'Sally had wanted me to see that Jed felt nothing for her. Huh! Sometimes the tension between the two of them was so taut you could have cut it with a knife.' Kirsten smiled in remembrance.

Jordanne smiled, too. 'And now they're happily engaged.' She sipped her coffee. 'Well, this is the first I've heard of these dinners.'

'You have been rather busy during the past few weeks. Maybe he just hasn't had the time to arrange it with you.'

'Perhaps,' Jordanne agreed, but somehow she doubted it. There was definitely something going on and Jordanne was going to find out *what*.

# CHAPTER TWO

ON FRIDAY afternoon, four full weeks since she'd started working with Alex, Jordanne was in her office preparing to go to the Institute of Australasian Sport to work on the research project. Her pager sounded and she glanced at the number. 'A and E,' she murmured, and sat back down at her desk.

'Dr McElroy,' she said once the connection was made.

'Jordanne, we have a private patient of Alex's here. Hit-and-run victim. Louise Kellerman.'

'I'll be right down,' Jordanne announced, and returned the receiver to the cradle. She contacted the Institute of Australasian Sport laboratory to let them know she probably wouldn't make it in that day before heading towards A and E.

'She's in trauma room one,' the sister there told her.

'Thanks.' Jordanne entered the room and crossed to Louise's side. She smiled commiseratingly at her patient. 'Are you feeling any pain?'

Louise's eyes closed momentarily before she looked at Jordanne, tears welling in her eyes. 'No,' she whispered.

'That's good. You're in good hands now. Everything will be fine. I'm just going to read the notes the paramedics have taken. You rest.'

Louise's response was to close her eyes. Jordanne felt strongly for the twenty-two-year-old woman who had only been to see her last Friday morning in Alex's private clinic.

She'd initially been to a skating rink and had been caught up in a gang of fast, enthusiastic skaters. They'd shoved her out of the way, sending her hurtling across the roller-rink into a collision with a wall. Her right femur had been fractured in two places. Alex and Jordanne had realigned the fractures before a cast had been applied.

Jordanne had been due to check on Louise's femur in another three weeks, and hadn't expected to see her patient until then. Now the poor woman had become the victim of a hit-and-run accident. Jordanne reviewed all of this in Louise's notes then read the paramedic report before receiving an update from Teagan Hughes, one of Alex's junior registrars.

'Ms Kellerman is stable and vital signs are good, which is amazing considering her injuries. Mild concussion and check X-rays will be requested. Left Colles' fracture to the wrist, fractured left humerus and her shoulder's been dislocated, too. Left hip is dislocated, left femur and tibia are fractured, and at this stage I don't know about her right femur. As you can see…' Teagan indicated the tatty cast that was being cut off Louise's leg '…the cast took quite a bit of damage. The paramedics said her crutches were in bits and pieces.'

'Disgusting. Hit-and-run accidents are disgusting,' Jordanne murmured. 'Go on.'

'The left side of her pelvis doesn't feel too stable so I was going to order X-rays for that as well.'

'Good. Let me know when she's out of Radiology. I'll tell Alex.' Jordanne checked on Louise, who was now sleeping, before leaving A and E and returning to the department. Alex was in a meeting and when she spoke to his secretary she discovered it was scheduled to go for at least another hour.

'Who's the meeting with?' Jordanne asked, wondering when would be a good time to interrupt it. Louise could well be another hour *just* in Radiology, depending on how busy they were.

'Your brother,' Alex's secretary responded.

'Jed?' Jordanne was surprised. 'Oh, well, in that case, I guess I *can* interrupt the meeting.'

She knocked once on Alex's door and opened it. Alex was sitting behind his desk while Jed sat opposite him. Both were laughing.

'Jordanne!' Jed's eyes lit up with happiness as he stood to embrace his sister.

'Hey, big brother.' She wrapped her arms around him in their usual family greeting. When she turned to face Alex his smile had disappeared and he was regarding her fiercely. What had she done *now?*

She stepped from Jed's arms and turned to face him. 'Sorry to break up the party but Louise Kellerman is in A and E. Victim of a hit-and-run accident.'

Alex groaned and looked at Jed. 'Can we finish this later?'

'Sure. When work calls...' Jed trailed off and a smile lit his face. 'Actually, it means I can go and surprise my fiancée while she's doing research this afternoon.'

Alex laughed. 'Time was we couldn't prise you away from your consulting desk, and now you're willing to play hookey? I knew I was right about you and Sally. Even before you met her you were so vehemently opposed to her.'

'Were you?' Jordanne asked her brother.

'It was Sally's wealthy background that made me... cautious,' Jed defended himself. 'Yet when Sally arrived in Canberra as my right-hand man, Alex immediately started flirting with her.'

'Really?' Jordanne was unable to hide her astonishment.

It seemed so out of character for the Alex Page she'd worked with over the past month.

Alex looked at her and shrugged before turning his attention to Jed. 'I knew if Jed had feelings for her they'd surface immediately—he was so passionate about disliking her, sight unseen.'

'That's a bit harsh,' Jed protested, his jaw clenching. 'I *never* disliked Sally.'

Alex smiled mischievously and the sight made Jordanne's breath catch in her throat. He was teasing her brother and loving every minute of it.

'And your engagement is proof of that. Admit it, Jed. If I hadn't shown any interest in Sally, you would still be pussyfooting around, trying to figure out which way was up. Instead, you're in love and you're happy.'

'You always like to be right,' Jed jested.

Jordanne looked from one man to the other. They really *were* very close friends, and for that reason alone she decided to make a bigger effort in getting to know Alex.

'Well, if you're both due elsewhere, I'll go and surprise my fiancée.'

'He just likes saying the word,' Jordanne said in a mock whisper to Alex, and for the first time Alex smiled directly at her. The full force of just how handsome he really was slammed into her and slammed in hard. Her knees began to wobble and she placed her hand on Jed's shoulder for support.

'See you soon,' she said, and reached up to kiss Jed's cheek.

'Tomorrow,' he agreed.

'What's happening, then?'

'Dinner at your brother's house,' Alex responded.

'That's right. Sally was going to invite you when she saw you at the IAS this afternoon but as you're not going…' Jed stopped. 'Tomorrow night—dinner at our house. Sally's inviting Kirsten, too, so the five of us should have a wonderful time.'

Jordanne glanced at Alex, realising he would be there as well. It was bad enough having to see him all day, every day at the hospital. She'd spent countless hours going over every conversation they'd ever had and especially that moment they'd shared in Outpatients earlier on in the week. Now she was going to be socialising with him at her brother's house? She shook her head slightly as she watched Jed and Alex shake hands.

Just seeing how different he was around Jed made Jordanne realise that after tomorrow night she'd be in for even more sleepless nights—dreaming of Alex!

'Retractor,' Alex ordered, and Jordanne complied. They'd been in Theatre now for almost five hours and Louise Kellerman had been stabilised. Once she'd finished in Radiology Alex and Jordanne had prepared for Theatre, and when Louise had been anaesthetised they relocated her left shoulder back into position as the X-rays had shown there was no fracture to the neck of humerus.

They'd also relocated her left hip, although the X-rays had shown a fracture to her left acetabulum. Her left femur had been stabilised in A and E but Alex and Jordanne fixed the fracture back with a G and K nail down the centre of the bone. Thankfully the cast had protected her other femur and a new cast was all that was necessary. Her left humerus required plating, and once that had been done they'd turned their attention to the open reduction and internal fixation of the Colles' fracture.

One aspect of her job that Jordanne had been amazed about was the way she and Alex worked together in Theatre. It was as though they'd been designed to complement each other, pre-empting what the other required without a word being spoken. As they realigned the bones of Louise's wrist, Jordanne smiled to herself behind her theatre mask. The operating theatre was one aspect of her job where Jordanne was more than happy for Alex to use monosyllables. She often did herself. Concentration was paramount and having to completely explain the procedure and requirements were distractions she'd rather not deal with whilst performing operations.

When the wrist was finished and both of them were happy with the check X-ray, they moved onto the tibia. Alex drilled a hole in the shinbone in order to secure a pin for the external fixator that was going to be attached to Louise's tibia. There were too many open wounds for a cast to be used.

For the next hour they worked solidly to attach the external fixator to Louise's tibia. Finally, everything was done and the patient was being wheeled to Recovery.

'I'll meet you in the tearoom and we can discuss Louise's pelvic X-rays,' Alex told Jordanne as he headed for the male changing rooms.

Jordanne changed and went to the tearoom, smothering a yawn on the way. When she arrived, she headed directly for the urn and made herself a cup of coffee. 'Would you like a drink?' she asked Alex as she stirred in some sugar, which she didn't usually have but felt she needed after *that* operating session.

'Black coffee.'

Jordanne was surprised. For some reason, she'd expected him to decline. She made him a cup and carried it over to where he was standing, looking at the X-rays on the viewing machine. She made sure their fingers didn't touch when she handed it to him.

'Thanks.' His gaze met hers briefly as he accepted the cup and placed it on the table.

Again she was surprised. Manners? Between the way he'd smiled at her in his office earlier and now a 'Thanks', her head was starting to spin. Jordanne felt her lips twitch into a small grin at this recent turn of events.

'Something funny?' he asked, glancing at her again.

'Nothing of consequence,' she replied, and took a sip. Jordanne closed her eyes, relaxing instantly as she swallowed the hot liquid. 'Mmm,' she groaned, and licked her lips. When she opened her eyes again it was to find Alex staring at her, a mixture of amusement and desire smouldering in the depths of his midnight blue eyes.

She watched as though in slow motion as Alex raised his free hand to her face. The instant his fingers made contact with her cheek Jordanne's breath caught in her throat, and when his thumb rubbed lightly over her parted lips a shiver of anticipation swept over her like a tidal wave.

Her heart hammered wildly against her ribs and she was positive he could hear it.

'So soft,' he murmured, before dropping his hand and turning his back to her.

Jordanne's mouth gaped open as she stared disbelievingly at the square set of his broad shoulders. A frown creased her forehead as she watched him remove an X-ray and put another one up.

'I think I'd like to leave the pelvis and take another set of X-rays in a few more days,' Alex said, not turning around to look at her.

'Excuse me?' Jordanne said, feeling her anger at his attitude beginning to mount.

'Surely you don't think we should operate now?' he asked, still not looking at her.

'I'm not talking about Louise Kellerman's X-rays, Alex,

and you know it.' She took a step forward and placed her cup on the table. She held her breath and counted to ten before saying more calmly, 'Look at me, please.'

At first she thought he wasn't going to comply but slowly he shifted slightly, his gaze meeting hers.

Under the penetrating effect that his blue eyes had on her Jordanne almost faltered—but not quite. 'Alex, you can't just caress my face, say how soft it is and then leave it at that.'

'Why not?' His expression was deadpan.

'Alex!'

'Jordanne!' he countered calmly.

She stopped and took another deep breath. 'There's…*something* going on between us. It has been since the first time we met. Don't try and deny it because your actions just testified to it.'

'All right, I won't deny it. I find you attractive.' He shrugged as though it was no big deal. 'Half of the male staff in the hospital find you attractive. It's simply a statement—you *are* an attractive woman.'

Jordanne was surprised at his words. 'I wasn't fishing for compliments,' she prompted.

'No?'

'Alex,' she ground out in exasperation, her temper beginning to bubble again.

'Look, Jordanne, we work together. Let's just leave it at that.'

Before she could say another word the door to the tearoom opened and Ian Parks walked in.

'What's the verdict on the Louise Kellerman's pelvis?'

'I'd like to leave it for a few days to see how it settles,' Alex told him. 'Are those her case notes?' Alex held out his hand for them.

'Yes.' Ian passed them over.

'Right. I'll go around to Recovery now and check on her progress.' With that, Alex walked out of the room without so much as a backward glance at Jordanne.

'Any water left in the urn?' Ian asked as he crossed to the sink. 'That was one involved operating stint.'

Jordanne just stood where she was, looking down into her cup of coffee.

'Jordanne?' Ian said a moment later, and she realised that he'd been talking to her.

'Sorry.' She turned to face him.

'Would you like another cup?'

'No, thanks.' Jordanne picked up both her own and Alex's coffee-cups and carried them over to the sink. She tipped the liquid down the drain, feeling as though it was some sort of symbolic gesture.

'Are you all right?' Ian asked.

'Just tired,' she sighed. 'It's been a long day.'

'Do you want to grab a bite to eat after we do a quick ward round?' Ian asked. When Jordanne hesitated slightly he added, 'Usually on a Friday afternoon some of the theatre and ward staff head over the road to the pasta restaurant. You've always been at the IAS on Fridays so we haven't been able to invite you before.'

Jordanne smiled and nodded, glad Ian wasn't asking her out on a date as she'd initially thought. After Alex's tossed out comment about half of the men in the hospital finding her attractive, she was feeling a little apprehensive. Going out to dinner with a group of people would definitely take her mind off Alex. Besides, the more friends she could make, the better chance she'd have of surviving this year working alongside her enigmatic boss.

Jordanne dressed with care the following evening, changing her mind at least five times. Eventually she settled on a pair of good denim jeans and a red knit top. She wanted to look casual but not too casual. Dressy but not too dressy. She brushed her hair out, letting it flow loose around her shoulders and down her back.

The last time Alex had seen her with her hair down had been the night she'd arrived in Canberra. Her brother Joel had been involved in a terrible skiing accident and Alex had been head of the retrieval team sent to rescue Joel. Jordanne could hardly remember her trip on the plane from Sydney to Canberra, except that the weather had been awful.

She sighed and looked at her reflection. 'Over a month ago,' she murmured. It seemed more like a lifetime since she'd first laid eyes on Alex Page. She brushed her hair with even more determination.

'That caress in the tearoom yesterday was definitely your cue to take things further,' she mused out loud. 'You're attracted to the man and he's attracted to you. Tonight you're going to make him realise that the attraction should be pursued,' she told herself with force, ignoring the small doubt that crept into her mind.

Jordanne checked her make-up and, satisfied with the result, she turned to find her bag. Her bed was covered with discarded clothes and she realised her bag was probably beneath them. Glancing at the clock, Jordanne groaned.

'You'll just have to dig it out and clean this mess up later,' she told herself sternly as she began hunting through the clothes. 'I really should make an effort to become a neater person,' she mumbled a second before she triumphantly closed her fingers around her elusive bag.

Hurrying into the kitchen of the small apartment she was renting for the duration of her twelve-month contract with Alex, Jordanne found the present she'd bought for Jed and Sally, picked up her keys and turned off the lights with her elbows. The cool September wind whisked around her the instant she set foot outside and she immediately re-thought leaving her hair down. Too late. She shrugged.

After the short drive to Jed's place, which was only two blocks from her own, Jordanne parked the car on the road behind Kirsten's old sedan. She'd been driving that car since med school and Jordanne smiled, remembering some of the camping trips and the old car which had faithfully taken them there. She, Kirsten and Sally had gone camping a few times after exams to let off steam and to get away from everything.

Sally's Mercedes was in the driveway but apart from that there were no other cars around, so she presumed that Alex hadn't arrived yet. As she raised her finger to the doorbell, Jordanne wondered whether he'd turn up at all!

Her question was soon answered. With her finger poised in the air a loud screech of tyres could be heard. She looked across the street to see a midnight blue Jaguar XK8 pull into the kerb. The driver cut the lights and engine before slipping from the car. Alex's movements were fluid, reminding Jordanne of a panther, as he locked the car and began walking towards her.

As she was standing illuminated beneath the front porch light Jordanne knew she had nowhere to run—even if she'd wanted to.

'Jordanne,' he said with a nod, his eyes quickly scanning her hair which was still being teased slightly by the wind.

Jordanne couldn't reply. Her mind was too busy registering how incredible he looked. He was dressed in black jeans, black shoes and a black jumper—sleek, suggestive and, oh, so sexy.

Her lips parted slightly as she allowed her gaze to slowly take her fill of him. Alex Page was becoming far too prominent in her life, her sluggish senses realised as her tongue slipped between her lips, wetting them. Jordanne clenched the present, bag and keys tighter in her hands.

Alex leaned insolently against the doorframe and hooked his thumbs into his jeans pockets as his gaze followed her lead. Jordanne's eyes widened in surprise but she couldn't have moved, even if she'd wanted to. He began at her sensible lace-up leather boots, travelled very slowly up her long legs, lingered briefly on her bust before visually caressing her lips. Jordanne felt a thrill of excitement course through her—as though Alex had actually reached out and touched her.

When his gaze finally reached her own, Jordanne knew the blue depths of her eyes were filled with desire. His sensual caress had left her feeling breathless and light-headed.

Neither seemed in a hurry to break eye contact. Jordanne shifted her stance, feeling as though her knees were about to give way at any moment, but she didn't drop her gaze. She leaned against the opposite side of the doorframe, marginally closer to Alex but still far apart.

'All right!' Jed yelled as he wrenched open the door, startling both Jordanne and Alex to stand up straight. 'Just press the doorbell once, Jordanne. There's no need to lean on it until the noise drives me insane.'

'Oh?' She looked at the button she'd inadvertently leaned against, then at Alex, then at Jed and back to the button again. 'Sorry, Jed.'

'Yeah, yeah,' her brother mumbled as he made way for them to come inside.

Jordanne tried to force her thoughts onto a more even keel and asked, 'Where's Sally? I have an engagement present for you.'

'She's in the kitchen,' he said as he ushered them into the living room. 'She's the one who's done most of the cooking tonight. Darling?' he called and went in search of his fiancée.

Kirsten was standing in front of the fire, looking at a family portrait of the McElroys that hung above the mantelpiece.

'Hi,' Jordanne said, and Kirsten spun around, her face lighting into a smile. They all greeted each other and Alex sat down on the lounge.

'Did Jed say Sally was cooking?' Jordanne asked Kirsten.

'You heard him correctly.'

'Why?' Alex asked.

'Sally doesn't cook,' Jordanne and Kirsten stated together.

'I see.' Alex smiled and rubbed his chin with his thumb and forefinger. 'This could be rather interesting. So, Kirsten, what have you been up to lately?'

Kirsten told him about the building project being undertaken at the back of her house. Jordanne was massaging her shoulder. 'We've spent the better part of the day painting.'

'I'm starting to feel my muscles complain,' Kirsten added.

'Have you finished?' Alex asked with a frown.

'Almost, but the outside still needs to be done.'

'Why don't you get someone else to do it?' Alex asked.

'Are you volunteering?' Jordanne queried.

'I meant pay someone to do it,' he clarified.

'Now he wants to charge you. He doesn't come cheap,' Jordanne quipped, and both she and Kirsten laughed.

'That's not what I meant,' he said with a smile. It appeared that tonight Jordanne was definitely going to see the side of Alex that everyone else had already witnessed. That of the cajoling, fun-to-be-around friend of her brother's.

'Hi, guys,' Sally said as she came into the room and embraced her new sister-in-law-to-be. Alex stood and kissed Sally's cheek.

'Congratulations again.'

'Thank you.'

'Rumour has it you're cooking dinner,' Jordanne said, teasing her friend.

'Yes,' Sally said proudly. 'Nothing flash but at least it's edible.'

'Sounds good.'

Jed came up behind Sally and placed his arms about her waist, drawing her close. 'I've had the best cooking teacher,' Sally pointed out as she turned her head for a kiss.

Jordanne sighed with happiness for her brother and her friend. 'I have a present for you both,' she announced, and handed over the beautifully gift-wrapped box.

'First one from Kirsten, now you. This wasn't supposed to be another engagement party.'

'I know but I couldn't resist.'

Sally carefully opened the present. 'Tea! How perfect.'

It was a wooden box with ten different teas in it. Considering that both Jed and Sally drank a lot of the beverage, Jordanne had thought they'd like it.

'We can sample some after dinner,' Jed suggested.

'I guess now it's my turn,' Alex said, and withdrew from the back pocket of his jeans an envelope. 'A small token— for you both.'

Jed took the envelope and opened it. There were some tickets inside and he looked at them before handing them to Sally.

'Thank you.' The two men shook hands.

'What is it?' Kirsten asked.

'A package to fly to Sydney, get picked up and chauffeured to dinner before going to the theatre.'

'You have the option to either stay overnight or fly back ready for a sunrise breakfast on the shores of Lake Burley Griffin here in Canberra,' Alex added. 'It's valid for twelve months so use it whenever you get the time.'

'It's terrific,' Sally said and kissed his cheek. Tears were brimming in her eyes. 'I can't believe I have such good friends and family.'

'Believe it,' Jordanne said, her own eyes filling with tears for her friend.

'I think this calls for champagne,' Jed announced, and with Alex's help soon they were all drinking a toast to good friends.

Jordanne glanced at Alex as she sipped from her glass and noticed that he was looking back at her. She felt a tingle of awareness travel through her body. Was there any hope of the two of them becoming more than just friends?

The evening progressed with a continued jovial air. Sally's spaghetti Bolognese was received with enthusiasm by everyone, especially Jed who was so proud of his fiancée he kept extolling her virtues until even Sally told him to be quiet!

In everything she did, Jordanne was very conscious of Alex sitting opposite her. Their gazes had met across the table several times and on each occasion Jordanne had felt a mass of tingles invade her body.

She was happy and enjoyed seeing this other side of Alex. After they'd had dessert and were relaxing in the lounge, sampling some of the tea from Jordanne's gift, Jed asked about work.

'So, how's my little sister been shaping up?' he asked Alex.

At Jed's words, Jordanne instantly thought back to the episode at the front door. It made her wonder just how she *did* shape up in Alex's eyes, especially after such a sensual caress.

Alex glanced briefly at Jordanne before looking back at Jed. 'Everything's fine,' he murmured, and sipped his tea.

'Come on, you've got to admit to more than that,' Jed persisted. 'Jordanne is an excellent surgeon and even though you were hesitant about creating the position of research fellow, you have to admit it was a brilliant suggestion on my part.'

Alex laughed at his friend's words, his gaze not meeting Jordanne's as he spoke. 'Yes, Jed. Absolutely brilliant. Thank you.'

'And now, as you work alongside Jordanne, you can almost experience at first hand what it's like to have a sister—well, surrogate sister at any rate.'

Jordanne looked at Alex. Was that the way he really saw her? As a surrogate sister? Or was that just how Jed perceived the situation?

Alex didn't reply to her brother's words but instead sipped his tea and commented on the taste of the blend. 'I love my coffee,' he said. 'But a nice cup of tea once in a while is as relaxing as a breath of fresh air.'

The conversation turned to comparing beverages and favourite foods, and after a few more minutes Alex's gaze finally met Jordanne's.

'I think I'll boil the kettle so we can try another one,' Jordanne suggested, and rose from the lounge. She looked pointedly at Alex and inclined her head towards the kitchen.

'Good idea,' Kirsten said as she looked through the box of teas.

Jordanne walked out to the kitchen, carrying a few of the dirty cups and saucers. She put them in the sink and waited. When Alex came in, carrying the rest of the cups, she didn't move. She leant against the bench, her arms crossed in front of her.

'Is that how you really see me, Alex? As some type of surrogate sister?'

'You're not one to beat about the bush, are you?' he replied as he placed the cups on the bench.

Jordanne didn't budge. 'Answer the question,' she pressed. He was silent as he filled the kettle and switched it on. 'Look, Alex, I have four brothers and I can tell you right now that none of them have ever made me feel the way you do. Big brothers don't go around caressing their little sisters with their eyes the way you did earlier tonight.'

He was silent for what seemed to be an eternity but which Jordanne knew was only a few seconds. When he spoke, his tone was solemn.

'I'm sorry about that, Jordanne. That was a big mistake.'

# CHAPTER THREE

FOR a brief moment Jordanne thought her heart had stopped beating. How could Alex possibly think that *anything* between them could be a mistake?

'No, it wasn't,' Jordanne countered emphatically, their voices still low so they didn't raise awareness from the other three people down the hallway. 'Yesterday, after Louise Kellerman's operation, was the first time you've ever indicated that you liked me, let alone found me attractive. The way you looked at me tonight was…' She trailed off as her breathing started to increase. 'It was so…sensual.' As she said the word Jordanne breathed out, her eyelids fluttering closed for a second. She opened them to find him studying her with that same look of desire that had been on his face yesterday. 'No one has *ever* made me feel that way before.'

'Jordanne—'

'Don't deny it, Alex. Despite whatever misapprehensions my brother may be under, our relationship is definitely *not* one of loving siblings. It's a relationship of one man and one woman who are undeniably attracted to each other.'

She kept her gaze glued to his, almost challenging him to deny it.

Alex looked down at the floor for a moment before returning to meet Jordanne's eyes. 'I told you yesterday that I was attracted to you. From what happened outside your brother's front door tonight, we both know that the attraction is mutual. What we *need* to focus on is that your brother is my best friend. For me to date you, Jordanne, regardless of what I feel for you, is just not on.' He lowered his voice even further. 'I'm sorry I looked at you the way I did.'

'Don't be. I enjoyed it,' Jordanne responded.

'Stop it, Jordanne,' he warned, but smiled nevertheless. 'There are many reasons why we can't get involved, and Jed being my best friend is one of them. I know I'll hurt you, and when I do it will ruin my friendship with Jed.'

'How can you possibly know you'll hurt me? You hardly know me, Alex.'

'I know enough. Look, Jordanne, you're headstrong and very independent. It's no wonder Jed wants to keep his eye on you. Regardless of this attraction we feel, it's going no further.'

Realisation dawned across Jordanne's pretty features. She smiled at him. 'So *that's* why you've been practically avoiding me during the past month.'

'I have not been avoiding you. We work together almost every day,' he protested.

'That's true but you made sure we were never alone for too long.'

He shrugged but didn't admit it.

'And all because you're afraid of my big brother!' she continued.

'That's *not* the reason,' he replied with a small shake of his head.

'I think you're lying,' she countered, still smiling. 'Alex, I know Jed is very protective of me but let's get one thing straight. If I'm attracted to a man and I want to start dating him, I don't ask *anyone's* permission except that of the man in question.'

'Well, if you're asking, the answer is *no*.'

'Why not?'

'Jordanne! Why can't you accept my response?'

'Because I don't believe it's the truth. I don't believe it would make either of us happy to deny this attraction. I come from a family that *embraces* happiness, Alex. You must know this from your friendship with Jed.'

'And it's a friendship that I value extremely highly,' he pointed out.

Jordanne nodded with understanding. 'So you'd rather not risk that friendship to find out what you and I might mean.'

'I guess you could put it that way.'

Jordanne looked at him for a long moment, realising he was struggling with emotions deep inside himself. 'OK,' she said thoughtfully. 'From now on, we'll be surrogate brother and sister. Purely platonic,' Jordanne announced as the kettle whistled before switching itself off. Jordanne turned to the sink and began rinsing the cups.

'Perhaps that's best,' Alex murmured, before returning to the others.

As they all drank tea and enjoyed themselves, Jordanne started to formulate a plan. She'd had years of practice at being a loving sister and she knew just how to get Alex to change his mind. Alex had witnessed the way she and Jed were around each other, and in the McElroy family it was their custom to be very demonstrative. Alex, as her new surrogate brother, was about to get a dose.

'So, Alex,' Sally said as she drained her teacup, 'Jordanne tells me you still haven't been out for your dinner yet. Too busy?'

Alex looked quickly from Sally to Jordanne and back again. 'Yes. As a matter of fact, we've been hectic since she started.'

'Hectic,' Jordanne agreed, and smiled sweetly at him. He gave her a cautious look but her smile simply increased.

Kirsten yawned. 'Oh, excuse me. I think it's getting close to my bedtime.'

'Me, too,' Jordanne agreed. Soon they were all collecting their belongings and saying their goodbyes. Jordanne embraced her future sister-in-law, thanking her for the lovely evening.

'Let me know what type of plan you're hatching to get Alex to come to his senses,' Sally whispered in Jordanne's ear. 'I'd love to help.'

Jordanne looked with surprise at her friend and then realised that she'd sadly underestimated her. Sally had never been one to be so totally absorbed in her own life that she couldn't see what was happening in others'.

'You're on,' Jordanne said softly, before turning to her brother. 'Thanks for a great night, bro,' she said, and soundly kissed him on both cheeks before hugging him close. 'Love you,' she said in his ear, and Jed returned her affection.

'We should do it again some time and soon,' he added.

'Great idea,' Jordanne agreed.

'Actually,' Alex said, after clearing his throat, 'as Jordanne and I haven't had our official dinner and as you all gatecrashed Sally's dinner, why don't you do the same for this one?' He turned to face Jordanne and raised an quizzical eyebrow. 'You don't mind, do you, Jordanne?'

'Uh…no. No, of course I don't mind. The more the merrier,' she said, knowing he'd only invited the others so he wouldn't have to be alone with her. The revelation made her feel triumphant that she had that type of power over him.

'How about next weekend?' Alex suggested. 'We're on call on Saturday so what about Sunday night?'

Sally and Jed looked at each other and nodded. 'Sounds great,' Jed responded.

'I don't have anything planned from what I can remember,' Kirsten agreed, giving Jordanne a quizzical look.

'Great. I'll organise it and let you know the details,' he said with a satisfied nod.

'It seems silly to all go in separate cars,' Sally piped up. 'Jed and I can pick up Kirsten as she's quite close. Jordanne, why don't you swing by Alex's house and pick him up?'

'Oh, no,' Jordanne replied, almost kissing Sally for her ingenuity. 'After seeing him pull up in that sporty Jaguar, I demand a ride as part of the dinner package!'

Alex laughed nervously.

'It's all settled, then,' Sally said. Jed held the door open, letting the cold wind in.

'Don't come out,' Jordanne said. 'Stay where it's nice and warm. Bye, and thanks again.'

'It was great,' Kirsten added.

'Drive carefully,' Jed called to all of them.

The three of them walked out to their cars. 'Now, which one was mine,' Jordanne said, looking from Kirsten's old car to Alex's new sporty one. Jordanne kept walking alongside Alex as Kirsten veered off. 'I think it's this one,' she said, crossing to the Jaguar.

Kirsten laughed as she unlocked her car. 'I'll call you later, Jordanne. Alex, it was great catching up with you.' With that, she got in her car, started the engine and drove off.

Jordanne waved, quite happy to stand by Alex's car. 'Now, what did I do with my keys?' she jested as she pretended to pat her pockets.

'Cute,' he said, and kept his distance—he at the rear of the car, she beside the driver's door.

'All right, I'll go. Thanks for an enjoyable evening, surrogate big brother,' she said lightly, and covered the distance between them. Jordanne knew she'd taken him by surprise as she wrapped her arms about his neck in a hug. Pulling him slightly off balance, he was forced to reach out and put his hands onto her waist. He dropped them the instant he regained his balance.

Jordanne reached up and kissed first one cheek and then the other—just as she'd done with Jed. When she'd finished she let her hands rest on his shoulders for a moment, their gazes locked, her face turned expectantly up to his own. Millimetres, she thought. A few more millimetres and their lips would touch, but brothers and sisters didn't kiss the way she was aching for Alex to kiss her.

She stepped back, gave his upper arm a playful tap and said, 'See you at work on Monday, *bro*.'

Jordanne walked across the road to her own car, fumbling with the keys. After she'd unlocked the door she turned to look at him again. He hadn't moved and was watching her with amazement at what had just transpired.

'Drive carefully,' she called, and climbed into her car. She had planned to toss a casual 'love you' in his direction, just as she would have to any of her brothers, but Jordanne knew that although she cared for Alex as a friend, to say the words, even in jest, would probably scare him off for good. She bit her tongue but settled for winding down the window and blowing him a kiss as she drove past.

Yep, by dinner next Sunday night, Alex would be begging her to stop playing sisters in favour of a more 'grown-up' game.

Alex was relieved when he let himself into his three-bedroom house later that evening. From now on he needed to keep one step ahead of Jordanne. He knew exactly what type of game she was playing with her surrogate sister act and he only had himself to blame. Instead of being cautious

around him—well, as cautious as Jordanne could be—she
was now going to be touching and hugging and kissing him
in front of people, just as she did with Jed.

'Why didn't I have a sister?' he grumbled as he crossed
to his answering machine. 'At least then I'd know how to
handle her.' The light was flashing once, indicating one
message. Alex pressed the button and waited as the tape
rewound itself.

'Alex, it's Scott. Was hoping to catch up. It's early morning here in Boston so give me a call when you get in. Just
some good news I wanted to share.' *Beep.*

Alex glanced at the clock—almost midnight. The perfect
time to call his brother in the States. The last time Scott
had given Alex some 'good news' it had been about his
move to the States. Alex had really missed his brother during the past two years as they'd always been and still were
good friends. He checked the number and dialled through
to Scott. The phone was picked up on the second ring.

'Hey, Scotty,' Alex said down the line.

'Alex, glad you got back to me.'

'Sorry. I've been out at a dinner party.'

'With a beautiful woman?' Scott teased.

'Not one—three, little brother.'

'Really? That's my bro—stud-muffin *extraordinaire*,'
Scott said laughingly.

'Not quite. It was dinner at Jed's house.'

'I thought Jed was engaged?'

'He is—we had dinner at his house with his fiancée, one
of his sisters and a friend.'

'I see. So who's the…friend?'

'Why are you so interested? You're a married man.'

'That's *why* I need to take a keen interest in *your* love
life.' Scott laughed.

'Garbage. You worship the ground Amy walks on. So,

what's your news?' Alex waited patiently for his brother to speak.

He heard Scott sigh. 'I don't know any easy way to break this to you so I'm just going to come right out and say it. I'm going to be a father—again.'

Alex felt his gut twist. Scott knew the truth of Alex's previous attempt at marriage and why it had failed.

'Congratulations, Scotty.' Alex forced a jovial air into his tone. After all, he *was* happy for his brother. 'When's the baby due?'

Scott was only three years younger than himself and already had two children in primary school.

'About two months after we return from the teaching exchange here.'

'Mum should be pleased. She'll have another grandchild to fuss over.'

'Yeah. I wanted you to hear it from me first, not Mum. I know it must be like a kick in the teeth to you—'

'Scott,' Alex interrupted. 'I'm glad you told me and don't worry about it. I'm happy for you and Amy—really I am.' He changed the subject and they talked about other things as well as how Alex's two nephews were doing in school. He had a talk to both of the boys before Scott came back on the phone.

Alex took a breath, knowing he wanted to ask Scott a question but not sure just how his brother would take it. 'Scotty? I know Amy has two sisters. How do you…get along with them?'

'Fine. Why?'

'No reason. I was just watching Jed with his sister to-night and they're all huggy and kissy—sibling stuff, you understand—and I wondered whether it's like that with your sisters-in-law.'

'Not really. Just a peck on the cheek when we see each

other, but Amy and her sisters are a different story all together. Hugs and kisses all round, and when their mother is about—well, look out! You could get smothered by all that emotion.'

Alex laughed. 'Thanks, bro. I needed to hear that.'

'Hey, aren't you working with Jed's sister?'

'Yeah.'

'So I should be asking *you* what it's like. Isn't Jed's sister just like the sister we never had?'

'That's what I'd anticipated.'

'She's not nice?'

'She's…nice.' Alex tried to keep any stray emotion of how he *really* perceived Jordanne out of his voice.

'What's her name again?' Scott probed.

'Jordanne.'

'That's right. So, Jordanne's…*nice*, is she? Not at all what you'd imagined for a surrogate sister, eh?' Scott chuckled.

'Look, Scott, it's getting late. I'd better go.'

'I've hit the nail on the head,' Scott crowed. 'So, should I brush off my tux?'

'Goodbye, little brother,' Alex said, and disconnected the call before Scott could say anything more. It was far too late to call his mother. He made a mental note to speak to her tomorrow and congratulate her on becoming a grandmother again. She would probably want to talk about how Scott's news had affected him, but in all truth he didn't really fancy rehashing the past. It had been seventeen years since he'd signed the divorce papers and Alex now felt that those memories belonged to someone else. He'd changed so much since then.

He focused on the present and Scotty's teasing remarks came to mind. He raked a hand through his hair as he stood. All he'd said had been that Jed's sister was nice. How could

Scotty have picked up on anything just from that one adjective?

Regardless of how he felt about Jordanne McElroy, any relationship between them was pointless and it had nothing to do with his friendship with Jed.

Monday morning saw Jordanne feeling on top of the world as she walked through the department to her office.

'You're certainly bright and cheery this morning,' Alex's secretary commented when they met in the kitchenette.

'Today is a new day.' Jordanne laughed as she made herself a cup of coffee. 'Is Alex in?'

'Yes. He wants a quick cup of coffee before ward round and clinic.'

'I'll take it to him,' Jordanne offered. 'You probably have a million things to do and I need to discuss Louise Kellerman with him.'

'Thanks, Jordanne.' She handed Jordanne Alex's cup. They walked up the corridor and after opening Alex's office door, his secretary left her to it.

Alex was concentrating on some paperwork as Jordanne walked across the carpet and placed the cup onto his desk.

'Thanks,' he murmured, without looking up, and Jordanne knew he thought she was his secretary.

'You're welcome,' Jordanne said, and loved the way his head jerked up at the sound of her voice. 'Can I type any letters for you?'

'Jordanne!'

'Ten points for accuracy.' She put her own cup on the table and came to stand behind him. 'So how are you this morning, *bro*?' She placed her hands on his shoulders and began to massage. 'Ooh, rather tense, I'd say. Not a good way to start the week.'

'Jordanne,' he warned, his voice low.

She bent down so her face was beside his. 'Yes?' she said softly in his ear.

Alex didn't turn his head to look at her because if he had their lips would definitely have met. Jordanne was glad he didn't. She didn't want to kiss him—not yet. As she'd thought through her plan yesterday, she was determined that when they finally kissed, Alex would be in complete control of the decision. She didn't want him regretting it the instant it was over.

'Thank you for the coffee,' he replied, and she straightened, laughing.

'Chicken,' she teased, but walked around the desk and sat opposite him, sipping from her cup.

'Was there something you wanted to discuss with me?' he asked, putting his pen down and reaching for his own cup.

'Louise Kellerman. I went down to the ward before I came up and she didn't have a good night. I don't think the pelvis is settling all that well.'

Alex nodded. 'We'll take a closer look after clinic. Thanks for bringing it to my attention.'

'You're more than welcome.' Jordanne stayed where she was, sipping her coffee.

'Anything else?'

'No.' She feigned innocence. 'Why? Am I bothering you? Is my presence making you unable to concentrate? None of my brothers have ever been bothered by me hanging around.' She shrugged. 'It's just what little sisters do.'

The corners of Alex's lips began to twitch and once again Jordanne marvelled at the difference a week had made where this enigmatic man was concerned. At least now that they'd both admitted there was an attraction between them, he wasn't trying to deny it any more.

'How long is this surrogate-sister act going to continue?' he asked.

Jordanne put her coffee-cup down and leaned right across his desk. 'As long as it takes,' she whispered seductively, and smiled widely as he swallowed convulsively at her words. 'Such a cute Adam's apple,' she crooned, before straightening. She took a few steps towards the door. 'Do we still have a meeting before lunch to discuss the research project?'

'Yes. Why would you think otherwise?'

'Just wondering whether you can trust me to be alone with you. That's all. All of our other meetings have included the pathologists and research staff out at the IAS. I'm glad you're not backing out.' She opened the door. 'See you in clinic, *bro.*'

Alex's secretary was right behind her as Jordanne made to go through the door. 'I didn't realise you and Alex were related,' she said as she walked passed Jordanne towards Alex's desk.

'Oh, we're not, but he's been friends with Jed for so long it's just like having another brother around. Isn't that right, Alex?' She smiled sweetly at him but went on before he could reply. 'You'd think I'd be satisfied with the four brothers that I have but...' Jordanne shrugged again '...one more won't make that much difference. I'd better get ready for ward round,' she said.

As it turned out, halfway through the clinic she needed to call Alex to review a patient who was requesting private coverage.

'Alex,' Jordanne said as he came into her consulting room, 'this is Mr Roberto Portatello.'

Alex shook hands with the patient who was sitting in a hospital wheelchair.

'Mr Portatello—'

'Roberto, please,' Mr Portatello insisted.

'Roberto,' Jordanne corrected, 'has been on the waiting list for a total hip replacement due to bad arthritis. His local GP put his name down here at the hospital some months ago but the situation is slowly getting worse. As you know, it will be at least another four if not five months before Mr...Roberto...' Jordanne smiled at him '...comes up for the hospital operating list.'

'I want to be private,' Roberto insisted. 'I can pay,' he verified.

'Do you have private health insurance?' Alex asked.

'Yes.'

'He forgot to tell his GP,' Jordanne added.

'Right, then. As you're here, we'll take a look at you before getting you organised onto my private operating list. Have you seen a rheumatologist?'

'That sounds scary,' Roberto replied. 'Is it a dangerous animal?'

Jordanne laughed. 'No. A rheumatologist is a doctor who specialises in arthritic cases such as yours. I think we can safely take that as a no,' she said to Alex.

'At this stage, you'll need an assessment from a rheumatologist before I can operate. We'll do a consultation now, refer you privately to the rheumatologist and then make another appointment for you to see me privately before the operation.'

'How long will all of that take?' Roberto asked sceptically.

'My private operating list is on a Thursday afternoon so hopefully a week next Thursday, we'll have you booked and ready to go.'

'So soon?' Roberto was amazed.

'Isn't that what you wanted?' Jordanne asked.

'Yes,' Roberto said, pleased.

'Let's get on with the examination, then,' Alex said with a smile. They took a good look at Roberto's hip and the X-rays he'd had taken that morning. 'I'll leave you with Jordanne to fix up the other details. All being well, I'll see you next Wednesday morning in my private practice, ready for your operation the following day.' With that, Alex shook Roberto's hand and left the room.

'What a good man,' Roberto praised after Alex had left. 'How long have you two been together?'

Jordanne frowned slightly at the question. 'We've been working together for a month now.'

'Ah!' he replied, and smiled knowingly. 'The romantic involvement hasn't progressed very far yet. That's good. Take your time with that one,' he advised.

Jordanne felt her face heat with embarrassment. 'What do you mean? Alex and I are just…friends,' she told her patient.

'For now.' Roberto gave her a careful stare. 'I've had a lot of experience in reading body language and I know the body language of two people who are romantically inter-ested in each other. Just don't rush him—or he'll turn tail and run the other way.'

Roberto's advice was exactly what Jordanne had sur-mised. She knew she was walking a very fine line with Alex. Still, her patient's comments piqued her interest. She looked at his chart, but under 'Occupation' it simply said 'Retired'. 'What was your profession before you retired?'

'I used to be a private investigator. It's this old hip that forced me out to pasture. Ageing isn't something I can do gracefully,' he told her with a chuckle. 'I turn seventy next year and, believe me, when I do, the whole world is going to know about it, I'll be grumbling and groaning so loudly.'

'That's the spirit,' Jordanne agreed. 'So, what type of cases did you previously work on?' She hoped to get him off the subject of herself and Alex. Thankfully, Roberto seemed willing to co-operate.

'A variety,' he replied. 'A lot of husbands cheating on wives—*and* vice versa. A bit of industrial espionage, medical benefits cases.'

'Where people are being paid out for an injury they don't have?' Jordanne was intrigued.

'That's right.' Roberto heaved a heavy sigh. 'My business had to be sold. Neither of my sons were interested in it. Both of them became chefs. My grandsons—not a scrap of interest amongst them either.'

'I'm sure you ran the best agency around,' Jordanne told him, and he nodded in agreement. She finished the consultation and was almost sorry to see Roberto go.

'See you next week,' he called as the orderly came to wheel him out of the consulting area.

'Ready for the next one?' Sister Trudy Elliot asked Jordanne.

'Almost.'

'Good.' Trudy started to leave but then came back. 'By the way, the hospital grapevine now knows about Jed and Sally's engagement. They were on call over the weekend,' Trudy explained. 'You nearly let it slip last week, didn't you? When I mentioned that Sally would have my head if I so much as looked at Jed.'

'Yes.' Jordanne smiled. 'I didn't want to spoil the surprise. Besides, it was up to them to make it known around the hospital.'

'It wasn't *that* much of a surprise as everyone knew they were dating. It was more a matter of time.'

Jordanne nodded and then asked rather hesitantly, 'Any more gossip about my family I should know about?' She looked down at the case notes on her desk, hoping to give the impression that she didn't really care.

'Not about your family. Just about you.'

'What?' Jordanne feigned innocence. 'What about me?'

'Just about your relationship with Alex.'

'We're colleagues,' Jordanne persisted.

'Yup.' Trudy nodded. 'The latest on the grapevine is that you view each other as brother and sister. After all, everyone knows what good friends Alex and Jed are. It therefore seems natural that he sees you as a sort of surrogate sister.'

'That's about the size of it,' Jordanne replied with a nod. 'I guess it's better than the previous rumour on the grapevine.'

'Which was?' Now Trudy *definitely* had Jordanne's attention.

'I guess everyone hoped you'd get together.'

'Why?'

Trudy shrugged. 'I guess because of the family connection. You know, Jed's marrying Sally who's his right-hand man. You're Alex's right-hand man. Alex and Jed are friends. It sort of just started from there. Besides, Alex is one of the most eligible bachelors in the hospital. Some of the nurses felt for sure that your McElroy good looks would bring him to his senses, but I guess not.'

'I guess not,' Jordanne repeated, feeling a bit desolate at the information.

'So now he's as free as a bird again, who do you think would be perfect for him? Ooh, I know, there's a new nurse on his ward.'

'Who?' Jordanne wanted to know.

'Oh no, she's engaged. What about Teagan Hughes? His junior registrar. She's pretty.'

'She's not his type,' Jordanne replied, instantly resolving to watch how Alex acted around Teagan.

'Well, you'd know.'

'Patients,' Alex snapped as he walked passed the open doorway where the women were chatting.

'Sorry,' Trudy called to his retreating back. 'Ready for the next one?' she asked again.

'Send them in,' Jordanne replied.

# CHAPTER FOUR

AFTER clinic, Jordanne went with Alex to the ward to review Louise Kellerman's pelvic fracture.

'How are you feeling today?' Jordanne asked as Alex picked up the chart at the end of the bed.

'The pain's not too bad.'

'Good.' Jordanne and Alex waited for the ward sister to shut the door of Louise's private room, before they continued.

'External fixator pin sites are slightly infected,' Jordanne commented as she gave the tibia a close inspection. She looked at Louise. 'That's unfortunately quite common but should settle down in a few days' time. I'll arrange more regular cleaning of the area.'

'Do we have the pelvic X-rays she had taken the other day?' Alex asked the ward sister.

'I'll go and check,' she replied, and left them alone for a moment before returning with the films. Alex held them up to the light and looked at them again.

'If you have a look here,' Alex said as he came around the bed and held the X-ray up for Louise to see, 'you can see the fracture to your acetabulum—that's the cup-like bone that the neck of the femur, your hip, fits into. I had hoped that the fracture might settle and heal itself, but as you're still experiencing discomfort I'd like to organise another set of X-rays to be taken. I'll also be requesting three-dimensional scanning of the pelvis so I can see exactly where the fracture is for when we take you to Theatre.'

'When will that be?'

'Depending on what the X-rays show, probably tomorrow morning if we can organise some time.'

'What do you mean, time?' Louise asked, a little worried.

Jordanne smiled reassuringly at her. 'Theatre schedules are more complex than any other timetable I've seen but, not to worry, we'll make sure there's time—should you need an operation.'

'Let's get these X-rays organised,' Alex told Jordanne. 'When we have the new views, we'll go through the operation with you so you understand exactly what's going on.'

'OK,' Louise replied. Alex gave her a quick smile before he and the ward sister went to fill in the paperwork. Jordanne stayed behind.

'Is there anything else troubling you?' she asked.

'It's just…everything.' Tears began to slide silently down Louise's face and Jordanne quickly reached for a tissue. 'My job, my home, my friends. How long am I going to be like this? Am I going to be able to have children after breaking my pelvis?' she sobbed as Jordanne wiped the tears from her cheeks.

'There's no reason why you shouldn't be able to have children. The bones of your pelvis will knit back together and be as good as new. I know it seems as though it will be ages before you feel your normal self again and I won't lie to you and tell you it will be any time soon. You've sustained multiple traumas—your body needs time to recover but I guarantee that in another twelve months you'll be surprised at how it's all passed so quickly.'

'Twelve months!' Louise burst into a fresh round of tears. 'I can't move my arm, or either of my legs. I have a catheter inserted and it's not that—'

'Comfortable,' Jordanne finished for her. 'I can imagine.'

'And then there's the police. Taking statements, asking questions.' Louise let a few more tears out. 'Have you ever been bedridden for a long time?'

'Not really. I broke my leg when I was ten.' Jordanne smiled at the memory. 'I fell out of a tree. I'm still not sure who my mother was more cross with, me or my brothers who'd tugged me up to the high branch.' The smile slowly disappeared as she looked at Louise. 'It *will* be all right. In time.' Jordanne instantly wished for her mother's natural soothing temperament but her sister Jasmine had inherited that. She willed the right words, which would make Louise feel more at ease, to spring into her mind. 'You've just got to give it time.'

Louise nodded her head and accepted another tissue. She tried to blow her nose with her right arm which was her only limb not bound in some type of traction or plaster.

'Even the simplest of tasks isn't easy,' Louise complained.

'I know,' Jordanne agreed softly. 'Hopefully, once we've fixed your pelvic fracture that'll be one less set of pillows and poking and prodding you'll have to endure.'

'How much longer am I going to be in?'

'For the pelvic fracture alone, it will be at least six weeks,' Jordanne told her. She and Louise had been through this before, but as so much had happened it was normal for her patient not to remember everything that had been said.

'My poor cat,' Louise groaned.

'I thought your parents were taking care of it?'

'They are, but I miss him.'

'Of course you would.' Jordanne was thankful that Louise seemed a bit calmer. 'I know it must be difficult for you. If there's anything I or any of the other staff can do to make things a bit easier for you—within reason,'

Jordanne added with a smile, 'then let us know. Unfortunately, we can't make you heal any quicker than your body will allow.'

'Thanks.'

'I read in your notes that you've spoken to the ward social worker. How did that go?'

'Dean? He's nice.' Louise looked down at her hands.

'Do you feel uncomfortable talking to him?'

'No. He's great. We can discuss anything—it's so strange. I thought I'd be inhibited with a man coming to talk to me.' She hesitated. 'I'm not that good with men. The guy who took me skating was a blind date and he didn't even accompany me to the hospital.'

'At least you feel comfortable talking to Dean. We need you to heal emotionally and mentally as well as physically,' Jordanne pointed out.

Alex came back into the room. 'X-rays are all organised and I've pulled a few strings to get you in immediately.'

'That's good news,' Jordanne agreed.

'The orderlies should be here soon to take you down to Radiology,' Alex told Louise. 'Jordanne and I need to finalise some things so we'll see you there.'

'Everything will be fine,' Jordanne said with a little squeeze of Louise's hand.

As they both walked towards Radiology, Alex asked, 'Is she all right?'

'She's just frustrated and a bit impatient.'

'I don't blame her,' Alex acknowledged. 'It's going to take quite a while for her to recover. Let's hope we don't find anything further with the three-dimensional scans. If it's just the acetabulum that needs piecing back together it will make it that bit easier on Louise.'

The scans of Louise's pelvis showed the fracture quite clearly and Alex was more than satisfied with the result.

'Get down to ESS Theatres and see what sort of theatre time you can get us. We'll need a good five hours at least to reconstruct that fracture. I'll meet you back in the ward.'

'OK,' she replied and headed for the emergency surgical suite. They couldn't reorganise the hospital elective list, even if they'd wanted to, as Alex's public operating session was on Tuesday afternoons and all of those patients had already been admitted to hospital that day.

As Louise was a private patient they could operate on her in a private hospital, but as her pelvic fracture wasn't stable Alex didn't want to risk moving her any more than necessary—and rightly so.

Jordanne didn't know the head nurse in ESS as well as she knew the staff in elective surgery but that didn't matter in this instance. She and Alex required theatre time for a patient within the next twenty-four hours and that was all there was to it.

Registered Nurse Colleen Pomeray was the theatre sister in charge, and Jordanne knocked firmly on her office door.

'Hi, Jordanne,' Colleen said, and motioned for her to enter. 'What can I do for you?'

'Take a guess,' Jordanne said as she came in and sat down opposite Colleen.

'Alex needs some theatre time.'

'Yes.'

'How much?'

'At least five hours. Acetabular reconstruction.'

'Is that for the hit-and-run accident who came in last Friday?'

'That's the one. Louise Kellerman.'

Colleen consulted her schedules. 'I can give you six hours straight in Theatre A tomorrow morning.'

'Excellent. I'll take it.'

'If I shift that case over there,' Colleen mumbled as she

rewrote the schedule, 'then move that case to an hour later then, *voilà*, six hours.'

'You're a gem.'

'I'd do anything for Alex,' Colleen said with a friendly smile. 'He operated on my sister four years ago and since then he knows he has me wrapped around his little finger.'

'Well I'm sure he'd be most grateful to you for accommodating this session. I know *I* am. At least I can take back some good news.'

'Tough day?'

'No tougher than others. At the previous hospital I worked at, a lot of the staff were unwilling to help out in situations such as these. It was like pulling teeth.'

'Sounds as though you're glad to be out of there.'

'My contract was only for twelve months—as is this one—and although they asked me to extend it, when Jed told me about the possibility of a job here I jumped at the chance.'

'So you like working with Alex?'

Jordanne grinned. 'Well, Alex is just like another brother to me.'

'He *is* a nice guy. Does he have any sisters?'

'No. Just one brother.'

'And now he has you?' Colleen asked.

'If we're to be completely accurate, I guess he has two. My sister Jasmine would have to adopt him as well.'

Colleen smiled. 'Sounds as though Alex is in for a new experience.'

Jordanne was about to quip something like, You've got that right, but decided against it. Instead, she said, 'Thanks for rearranging things. I'll go tell Alex the good news.'

As she walked towards the ward, Jordanne wondered how well Colleen Pomeray knew Alex. The thought made

Jordanne very uncomfortable. Imagining Alex with another woman, it made her stomach lurch and twist into knots.

As she rounded the corner into the ward, Jordanne forced the issue from her mind. She'd discuss it with Kirsten later. She found Alex in the nurses' station, laughing at something Teagan Hughes had said. The way the registrar was looking at him—like the cat who'd got the cream—reinforced the knots in Jordanne's stomach.

Had the staff behaved like this towards him during the past month? Was it something new Jordanne was seeing or had it always been there? Jealousy began to rear its ugly head but she forced herself to quash the emotion. She was the one who'd started this surrogate-sister business and now she had to acknowledge that Alex might be playing his own games.

She pasted on a smile as she walked into the nurses' station.

'Am I the best, or am I the best?' she asked rhetorically.

'You've arranged theatre time,' Alex guessed, turning his gaze from Teagan to her.

'Exactly. Six vacant hours of ESS theatre time tomorrow morning is now booked for Louise Kellerman.' Jordanne smiled up at him and he returned the smile. She felt warmed and once again had confidence in her plan. The lump of lead in her stomach returned to its usual fluttering of butterflies. Amazing how a simple smile from the man could completely change her attitude.

'Good. Let's check on Louise before getting the equipment organised.' They walked to her room and did a final check on her operation sites before leaving her to doze in peace.

'Are you going?' Teagan asked, and Alex nodded. 'Well, then, I guess I'll see you tomorrow night, if not before.' She smiled at him again as he and Jordanne left the ward.

The lead returned. 'Tomorrow night?' Jordanne queried, trying to keep her tone impartial.

'Uh-huh.' Alex nodded as they headed back to his office, Louise's latest set of X-rays under his arm.

'What's tomorrow night?'

They came to the door of the department and Alex stepped forward to hold it open for her. His grin was like that of the Cheshire cat and Jordanne had the distinct impression he was up to something. 'Nothing in particular,' he replied casually, and headed for his office.

Jordanne stopped by her own office and removed her white coat and stethoscope. Both of them had a theatre task force committee meeting in another hour and Louise Kellerman's theatre equipment was their first priority. What she'd really like to do now was to drag him out of the hospital and take him somewhere quiet where they could talk.

Roberto Portatello's words came instantly to mind. 'Don't rush him,' she whispered softly to herself, and knew that when she entered his office she'd be the calm, controlled, consummate professional that he'd hired.

Jordanne walked to his office and found the door slightly ajar. As he was expecting her, she didn't bother knocking but instead walked in and closed the door. Her new resolve crumbled the moment she looked at him.

Alex was sitting in his chair, his eyes closed and his fingers gently rubbing his forehead. Jordanne crossed quietly to his side and placed her hands on his shoulders. She'd only been pretending to massage them this morning but now, after his initial shock at her touch, she urged him to stay still.

'Try and relax,' she said, dropping all pretence. She stood behind his chair and kneaded his knotted-up shoulders. Neither of them spoke for at least ten minutes while Jordanne's fingers worked their magic.

'Better?' she asked as she came around his desk.

Alex opened his eyes and gazed at her. The blue depths didn't radiate anything other than fatigue. It was as though he was letting her glimpse the *real* man who lived deep down inside his soul. 'Thank you.' The two words were said without any pretence or double meaning and Jordanne accepted them like a precious treasure.

'You're welcome.' She reached for the packet of X-rays he'd put on the table and took them over to the viewing box. 'We'll have to shelve our discussion of the research project until later,' she said. 'As we don't have much time now, let's get started.'

They discussed the scans in detail, going over what approaches to use and what instrumentation and equipment would be required. Finally they were done but were running late for the meeting.

'I'll go to the meeting if you wouldn't mind organising the equipment. Also, would you mind telling my secretary about the operation and asking her to cancel my morning meetings?'

'Sure.'

'What did you have planned for tomorrow morning?' he asked as he shrugged into his suit jacket and picked up the necessary theatre task force committee file from the desk.

'I had a few interviews scheduled for the research project but I can rearrange them for Friday afternoon.'

'Was Dylan Foster one of them?' he asked with a frown.

'Yes.'

She had expected him to start on another tirade of her being careful or of him wanting to be there when she interviewed Dylan. Instead, Alex simply nodded and headed for the door.

'I'll come to the meeting as soon as I've finished.'

'Don't rush,' he said with a smile. 'They're never that exciting.' With that, he walked out, leaving her standing in the middle of his office.

It took a moment or two for Jordanne to get over the effects of his casual smile. She wished he wouldn't unleash them on her without warning. Gathering the X-rays together, she stopped by his secretary's office to pass on the message before heading back to ESS.

Jordanne knew she was in grave danger of falling in love with Alex Page, and at this moment in time she wasn't at all sure that she wanted to stop it.

'Suction,' Alex said and then added, 'Let's get this final reconstructive plate and screws in and we'll be ready for a check X-ray.'

They'd already inserted a reconstructive plate through the anterior approach and now, through the posterior approach, another reconstructive plate was required.

'Good,' Alex told his staff once they'd completed the task. 'Check X-ray, please.'

Once this had been done and both Jordanne and Alex were satisfied with the fracture's reduction, they began to close in layers. It wasn't too much later that Louise was being wheeled to Recovery and Alex sat down to write up the operation notes.

Jordanne went to the female changing rooms, deciding it wasn't worth changing out of theatre clothes for now as they still had the hospital's afternoon operating list to get through. She brushed her hair and wound it back into a bun before checking the clock. Just enough time to grab a bite to eat. If they started their elective operating list late, there'd be trouble.

As Jordanne was coming out of the changing rooms, she

saw Alex going into the male ones. He looked at her and smiled. 'Going to get some lunch?' he asked as he stood in the doorway.

'Yes. I'll check on Louise first. Can I get you anything from the cafeteria?'

He thought for a moment before saying, 'Just save me a seat. Thanks to the hospital grapevine considering us almost brother and sister, I guess it's OK for me to sit and eat lunch with you.' Before she could reply he continued, 'I must say how amazed I am that such a rumour has spread so quickly around the hospital. I can't imagine where it originated.'

'Can't you?' Jordanne asked with a sweet smile on her face. 'Neither can I.' They looked at each other. The silence seemed to stretch on for ever as neither of them spoke, at least not with words. Alex's deep blue eyes could be *very* expressive, and the more Jordanne looked into them the more adept she became at interpreting the unspoken language that seemed to be developing between them.

The smile slowly disappeared from her face as she saw desire spark in the depths of his gaze. The world around them seemed to blend into obscurity as she looked from his eyes to his mouth and noticed that he wasn't smiling either. Jordanne had fantasised too many times to count how incredible she knew she'd feel the very first time Alex kissed her. She swallowed again and parted her lips, unable to breathe properly. Her knees were beginning to fail in their job of holding her steady.

All she wanted was for Alex to grab her by the shoulders, spin her into the male changing rooms, thrust her up against the wall and plunder her mouth with his own. A shudder cascaded over her at the thought.

From the look in his eyes, it appeared that Alex was thinking along similar lines. Jordanne knew that if she simply stepped up onto tip-toe she'd be well within kissing distance. She also knew that the time wasn't quite right. To kiss Alex now would jeopardise any hope of them becoming more serious in the future—and that was what Jordanne now desperately wanted more than anything. To see what would evolve if they both gave it enough time and attention.

Instead of stepping in closer, Jordanne eased away and dropped her gaze. She nipped her bottom lip between her teeth and closed her eyes for an instant. Opening them again, she took a deep breath and took another step back. Forcing a smile, she said, 'I'll…um…' She stopped and cleared her throat, knowing full well that her voice sounded extremely husky. 'I'll save you a seat. Coffee?'

'Great,' he replied, also with a forced smile. Any earlier camaraderie they'd managed to obtain had been blown away with the wind after that near kiss. Or, Jordanne thought as she turned and walked down the corridor, a near *miss*.

As it was the beginning of the lunchtime rush, Jordanne quickly joined the queue and bought some sandwiches. Then she crossed to the tea and coffee facilities, which were complimentary and available twenty-four hours a day, and made two cups of coffee. Black with no sugar for Alex and white for herself. Finding a seat was about to become an impossibility, but she managed to get a table where there were four seats vacant.

Sitting down, she tried not to scan the doorway for Alex. He'd said he'd come so all she could do was wait. Jordanne unwrapped the sandwiches and bit into one. She'd eaten three before he walked in and she couldn't remember what any of them had tasted like.

As he scanned the cafeteria, looking for her, Jordanne became paralysed. When his gaze finally settled on her, she smiled despite the fact that she was desperately trying to get herself under control again.

'Calm down,' she told herself softly, and managed to quash the fluttering butterflies in her stomach. 'Hi,' she said when he was a bit closer. Alex slumped into the chair opposite her.

'It's been ages since I've ventured into the cafeteria during the lunchhour rush.'

'I know what you mean.' Jordanne laughed. 'I was in here last week and almost had to call for an ambulance it got so crowded. Here…' Jordanne motioned to the cup of coffee. 'Have a sip of this and you'll begin to feel better.'

He did as she suggested and looked at her over the brim. 'You remembered,' he said softly after swallowing.

'Black—no sugar,' she replied, knowing exactly what he was talking about. Again their gazes held and Jordanne was beginning to think she couldn't control the rate in which a relationship might develop between them.

'Mind if I sit down?' Ian Parks asked as he slumped into the chair next to Alex. 'How did Theatre go this morning?'

Alex looked at him as Jordanne took a sip from her cup.

'Quite well,' he answered. Ian started talking about his morning and discussing a few of the cases currently in the ward. Within five more minutes Teagan Hughes had joined them and together the four of them ate lunch. In some ways Jordanne was glad of their company. It meant that she and Alex *could* be seen together around the hospital without raising too many eyebrows. In other ways she wasn't so happy. Teagan kept looking across at Alex and smiling at him a lot.

All too soon Alex announced it was time for the elective theatre list. He and Jordanne said their goodbyes to Ian and Teagan.

'Oh, I'm coming with you,' Teagan said, smiling warmly

at Alex. 'As one of your junior registrars, I believe it's part of the orthopaedic training programme that we're taught by the senior consultant in operating procedures.'

'Quite right,' he replied, and gave her a small smile that didn't quite reach his eyes. 'Let's go, then.'

The three of them walked towards Theatre. As both Alex and Jordanne were already in theatre garb, they checked their list and went to speak to the patients. Teagan came in after changing and seemed a bit miffed that Alex hadn't waited for her.

'It doesn't matter,' Jordanne pointed out, trying to be positive towards Teagan. 'Let's get scrubbed. We have a busy list to get through.'

There were two knee arthroscopies and one removal of surgical metal. Once more Jordanne and Alex worked like a well-oiled machine and the theatre list proceeded without a hitch. As Jordanne degowned, she was thankful the day was almost over.

She waited until Alex had finished writing up the operation notes before they checked that all three patients were nicely stabilised in Recovery.

'Let's get down to ESS,' Alex said, trying to smother a yawn.

'Agreed,' Jordanne said, equally as tired.

'Why do you have to go down there?' Teagan asked with a frown. 'Surely you don't have *more* operating to do?'

'No,' Alex replied with a small smile. 'Our clothes are in the ESS changing rooms.'

'Oh.' Teagan nodded. 'Well, don't forget tonight,' she prompted.

'I won't,' he replied, and with a smile still in place he gave her a nod before turning towards the doors that led out of the elective theatre block.

Jordanne had watched him closely through out that brief

exchange. As before, when he'd been talking to Teagan, the smile didn't quite meet his eyes and she had the distinct impression that although he liked the junior registrar, he had no romantic feelings towards her. At least, she *hoped* that's what it meant. He *was* very tired, so it might be fatigue that was causing him to be less enthusiastic.

Regardless of what she might have perceived, she still felt her stomach twist into knots at the mention of him seeing Teagan Hughes after hours. He knew this surrogate brother and sister business was all an act. He'd admitted to finding her attractive and that he didn't think they should pursue it. That didn't mean that he should flaunt his love life in front of her.

Jordanne ground her teeth together as she followed him down the stairs and along the corridor that lead to ESS.

'You all right?' he asked.

'Why?'

He shrugged. 'You're just quieter than usual.'

'You should be so lucky. I thought you'd be enjoying the reprieve.' Jordanne tried to force a jovial air to her words but knew they also sounded clipped. They walked down the small corridor where the ESS changing rooms were located. There was no one else around. Alex put his hand on Jordanne's arm and stopped her.

'Tell me what's wrong,' he demanded.

'It's nothing.'

'Come on, Jordanne,' he cajoled. 'You can tell me. I'm your *brother*.'

'Ha.' She laughed without humour and sighed. He was right, though, and she was annoyed with herself for feeling weak. She raised her gaze to meet his. 'Where are you and Teagan going tonight? She seems determined to let everyone in the hospital know that you're seeing each other after hours.'

Alex raised his eyebrows questioningly. 'Just like you were eager to let the hospital know we're almost "family"?'

Jordanne nodded. '*Touché.*'

Alex placed a hand on her shoulder and looked into her eyes. Jordanne commanded her knees to stop weakening and to hold her up. She wished Alex would give her warning when he was going to touch her—at least then she could prepare her senses against the onslaught of emotions that coursed through her body every time he came close.

'Teagan and I are going to a dinner meeting tonight with two of the teaching staff from the med school. She wants to start her Ph.D. now and has asked me to discuss it with her old lecturers, one of whom has volunteered to be her supervisor.'

'That's a lot of extra work she'll be taking on,' Jordanne pointed out with a frown.

'I'll be raising that point tonight. She has three years left on the orthopaedic rotation and the work level is going to quadruple.'

Jordanne nodded, clearly remembering her own final year.

Alex squeezed her shoulder lightly. 'There's nothing more going on between us.' He looked down into her up-turned face and slowly, ever so agonisingly slowly, his head began to close the distance towards her own.

Jordanne's eyelids fluttered closed and her lips parted slightly in anticipation as she tried desperately to control the rapid increase of her heart rate. Finally, with a softness that tipped her over the edge, Alex's lips brushed against her own.

# CHAPTER FIVE

AT THE sound of someone clearing their throat, Jordanne and Alex sprang apart like two guilty teenagers caught kissing behind the school shed.

Jordanne's wild eyes focused on Colleen, the sister in charge of ESS.

'I think I'll get changed,' Alex said, and pushed open the door to the male changing rooms. He was gone in a flash. Jordanne followed his example and went into the female changing rooms. She was at her assigned locker, hoping that Colleen wouldn't follow her but knowing the theatre sister would.

'So you two are like brother and sister?' Colleen said with a wide smile on her face.

Jordanne concentrated hard on taking her clothes out of the locker. 'Brothers and sisters kiss,' she pointed out.

'Not like *that*,' Colleen said with a chuckle. 'Look, Jordanne, I promise I won't say anything. What you and Alex do is your business. If it's easier for the two of you to be seen together around the hospital pretending to be brother and sister, that's fine by me.'

Jordanne started changing, glad that Colleen wasn't going to spill the beans.

'Although,' she added thoughtfully, and Jordanne quickly looked up at her, 'I might charge you a fee for my silence.'

'You're going to *blackmail* me?' Jordanne asked incredulously.

Colleen's smile increased and she nodded. 'I want to know exactly how long this has been going on.'

Jordanne frowned. 'That's it? That's your fee? I have to answer a question?'

'That's it, but be careful where you kiss next time. So? Answer the question.'

'I'm afraid you're going to be disappointed. There *is* something between Alex and myself and we've acknowledged that, but as for being a couple—no. That was the very first time he's *ever* kissed me.'

'And I interrupted it. Sorry.'

Jordanne could tell that Colleen was truly sorry. She put her shoes on. 'Never mind. We're having dinner on Sunday night—'

'Great.'

'With three other people,' Jordanne finished.

'Not so great.' Colleen grimaced.

'No, it's fine, but thanks to the suggestion from my brilliant sister-in-law-to-be, Alex will be driving me and picking me up.'

'More time alone and in a more private place than a hospital corridor.'

Jordanne took the pins out of her hair and shook it free. Reaching for her brush, she worked the knots out.

'Wow! Your hair is gorgeous. Has Alex seen you like this?'

Jordanne smiled. 'A few times. It's starting to become one of my greatest assets.'

'Use it,' Colleen agreed. 'Leave your hair down and perhaps he'll take you out to dinner tonight.'

'He has a meeting,' Jordanne explained as she closed the locker door and picked up her bag. She put her theatre clothes in the basket beside the door. 'Thanks for being so nice about this, Colleen.'

'My lips are sealed,' she promised. The two women walked out of the changing rooms together and down to the ESS doors. There was Alex, leaning against the wall, waiting patiently for her.

Jordanne had half expected Colleen to make some sort of comment or a wisecrack, but instead she waved to Alex and called, 'See you later.' Then she turned and headed back to her office.

'Everything OK?' he asked as he straightened up. His gaze rested on her loose hair before returning to meet her eyes.

'Fine.' She nodded for emphasis, glad she'd left her hair down. 'I thought you might have left already.'

Alex shook his head. 'I'll walk you to your car. It's dark now,' he added by way of explaining his presence.

They walked out of the hospital in silence, the wind teasing the ends of her hair.

'Busy day,' Alex said after a while.

'Hectic,' she agreed. She wasn't sure what to say to him and although she was happy that he'd finally kissed her, Jordanne now felt a little uneasy.

That was all they said until they reached the doctors' car park. He walked her to her car and waited while she unlocked it. The wind once more breezed through her hair and Alex reached out to smooth it back from her face.

'Beautiful,' he murmured as he ran his fingers through its length. He looked down into her eyes. 'Jordanne, we need to talk.'

All Jordanne could do was nod.

'I wish I didn't have this meeting tonight, but if I cancel I'll just have to reschedule.'

She nodded again. 'Better to get it over and done with.'

They looked into each other's eyes for a few more seconds before Alex took a small step away. Jordanne belatedly realised she'd been holding her breath, willing him to kiss her once more, but it wasn't to be.

'Drive carefully,' he said, and turned to walk towards his own car.

Jordanne climbed behind the wheel of her car and went through the motions of driving. When she arrived home, she sat down and thought over everything that had happened. Usually, when some minor breakthrough had happened with Alex, she'd be on the phone to Kirsten like a shot. Tonight, however, Jordanne didn't really want to discuss it with anyone. She wasn't sure how Alex would react now, after their kiss—extremely brief though it had been. He'd said he wanted to talk and Jordanne dreaded it. She was positive he'd say it had been a mistake.

The only thread she had to hold onto was that *he* had been the one to instigate the kiss. She sighed and clung to that knowledge for dear life.


The rest of the week proved to be more hectic than Jordanne had anticipated as they both had extra work from Tuesday that they had to catch up on.

By late Friday morning, as they completed the clinic at Alex's private practice, Jordanne was ready for a holiday. She massaged her temples, hoping her headache would go away but there was only one way for that to happen—by finding some time to talk to Alex. She'd hardly slept a wink since that kiss three days ago and as his attitude towards her had been overly polite, coupled with monosyllables, Jordanne was almost positive that when they *did* find the time to talk, he'd tell her it could never happen again.

The only bright spark in her week so far had been Louise Kellerman's recovery. Thankfully, she'd not had any further complications after her pelvic fracture surgery. The reports from the physiotherapist and occupational therapist, as well as the social worker, on her condition had all been quite satisfactory. Her drains had been removed and the bruising from the accident had reduced dramatically. When Jordanne had seen her this morning, Louise had been in quite optimistic spirits.

When the last patient had gone, Jordanne typed up the notes, saved her documents and switched the computer off.

She took her empty coffee-cup back to the kitchen and was in the process of rinsing it when she felt rather than heard Alex come in. She kept her back to him and made sure the cup was *really* clean. Jordanne knew that if she turned around, she'd either throw herself into his arms or rush out of there in tears. Her emotions were strung taut like a drum, her shoulders knotted with tension.

'All done?' he asked.

The smooth silkiness of his voice washed over her and Jordanne momentarily closed her eyes. The cup was squeaky clean now and she could tell he was waiting for her to face him.

Jordanne reached for the teatowel and slowly turned to look at Alex. She leaned against the bench for extra support.

'Yes.' Her tone was slightly clipped.

He held out a piece of paper. 'This is a letter from Roberto Portatello's rheumatologist. He said he's fine for surgery so everything can proceed as planned.'

'Good.' Jordanne forced a smile. She looked down at the cup she was drying.

'You know, Jordanne,' he said in that, oh, so sexy voice of his that made her want to melt into his arms, 'if you rub that cup any harder, the pattern will come off.'

Jordanne didn't smile. He was trying to lighten the mood but just the sound of his voice and the way it made her feel was starting to exhaust her.

'Have you got some time now?' he asked, putting the letter on the table. Their gazes met and locked. Jordanne's heartbeat increased rapidly and she leaned further against the bench as her knees began to buckle. The deep blue of his gaze was something she should be used to by now but Jordanne was certain that even if she could look into those eyes every day for the rest of her life they'd still affect her in the same way.

She knew in that split second that she was definitely in love with the man. He was everything she'd ever dreamed of, he complemented her in every way and he'd captured her heart for ever. Alex Page *was* her Mr. Right.

The thought that she'd actually found him astounded her. In this wide world of people, her soul mate was standing right in front of her. He'd been her brother's best friend for over a decade and here he was, asking her if she had some time to talk.

With the revelation of her true feelings towards Alex, Jordanne wasn't at all sure what to do. She was positive Alex would say the brief but incredible feel of his lips brushing against hers had been a mistake. That they shouldn't pursue the attraction that almost erupted like a volcano whenever they were near each other. If he'd thought otherwise, why hadn't he just grabbed her and kissed her every day since it had happened? After all, it was all she'd wanted.

Her lips parted but she found that she couldn't speak any words. She knew he was watching her carefully, trying to decipher her expressions.

'Jordanne.' The word was said softly, almost a caress, and for one fleeting millisecond Jordanne thought she might have a chance.

The ringing of her mobile phone startled her so much that Jordanne dropped her coffee-cup. *Crash!* She looked down at the pieces of porcelain that had shattered all over the kitchen floor before snatching the phone from her waistband.

Turning to face the sink, she spoke harshly into the receiver. 'Yes?' She listened intently to the person at the other end. 'Right. I'll be there soon. Thank you.' She disconnected the call and hung her head. Taking a deep breath, she tried to relax her body. It didn't work.

'That was the IAS. Apparently Dylan Foster has turned up early for his appointment with me this afternoon.' Jordanne spun around only to find Alex crouching on the floor, cleaning up the mess with a dustpan and brush.

'I'll take care of this,' he told her. 'You'd better go start your afternoon research session.'

Jordanne felt worse than she had before. One single action from him would wipe away all the stress within her. With one little reassuring kiss, no words would be necessary. He inclined his head towards the door when she didn't move.

'Right. Thanks,' she said, remembering her manners as she walked past him and out of the room. Why did it feel as though she were walking out of his life?

Jordanne forced herself to concentrate on the traffic during the short drive to the IAS. When she arrived, she was glad to see that Dylan Foster's wife had accompanied him. Jordanne was in no mood to be evasive and polite if Dylan Foster tried any of his pick-up lines on her.

'These X-rays look good,' she told him after she'd reviewed the new set of films he'd had taken a few hours ago. It was part of the study to take check X-rays of the fractures to see precisely how they were healing.

'Now I need to take a small sample of blood for testing and then I'll explain again about the medication you'll be taking.'

Jordanne tried not to smile as Dylan paled at the sight of the needle. 'Perhaps you should lie down,' she suggested. When he was lying on the examination couch, Jordanne motioned for his wife to come over, too. 'Would you mind talking to your husband, Mrs Foster?' she asked softly. 'Distract him a little?'

'Sure.'

Everything was going fine. Jordanne swabbed his arm and rechecked that the tourniquet was tight. She'd inserted the needle and was almost finished when Dylan turned his head to see what she was doing and promptly passed out.

Jordanne withdrew the needle and quickly dealt with the blood before washing her hands. 'Dylan?' Jordanne called, and he slowly roused. 'Just as well he was lying down,' she said softly to his wife, who smiled.

'He hates the sight of blood,' Mrs Foster stated. 'He's hopeless when the kids cut themselves. I don't know why he looked.'

'Never mind. Just lie there for a while, Dylan, and you'll soon be feeling as right as rain.' She gave him a drink of water which he sipped with his wife's help.

When he was feeling better, Jordanne checked his blood pressure and pulse before allowing him to get off the couch. He hobbled over to the chair and sat holding onto his wife's hand as though his life depended on it.

'Right, now I'll just go through the medication with you again.' She handed his wife a small plastic bottle that had one hundred tablets in it. 'You need to take one tablet per day, preferably around the same time of day and after food.'

'So it doesn't matter when, just the same time,' Mrs Foster clarified.

'Yes. As I explained before, the tablets are a new non-steroidal, non-performance-enhancing medication. The study has two sections, people who have recent fractures, that is, less than six months old, and people who fractured their legs more than six months ago.

'What the medication does is to repair small fractures, stress fractures, hairline fractures—that sort of thing—without requiring surgical intervention. When a bone is fractured, bone-building cells called osteoblasts help to remodel the bone. This medication assists the formation of not only the osteoblasts but other cells involved in bone regeneration, thereby helping the smaller fractures to repair themselves more quickly.'

'Why?' Mrs Foster asked.

'Once the smaller fractures are healed, the bone becomes stronger, thereby allowing better health to the patient and faster regeneration of larger fractures.'

'So the aim of this research study is to test whether this medication really works in the way you've just told me?' she asked. Dylan was still fairly white and wasn't up to asking questions.

'Yes.'

'You said previously that your research was mainly on athletes.'

'That's right. Athletes have a higher rate of injury and re-fractures are more common, but to round the study out we wanted to test not only professional athletes but amateur athletes and non-athletic people. Most of the athletes I'm seeing have old fractures so we're hoping to prove that the medication helps strengthen the bone and guard against re-fracturing. With Dylan's history of being an amateur athlete, as well as re-fracturing the same bone as he's done, it makes him a unique candidate for this study.'

'There you are, dear.' His wife patted his hand. 'Someone thinks you're unique.'

Jordanne tried not to smile at her words. She handed Mrs

Foster a card. 'Here are my details. This is my answering service and if I'm not available, leave a message with them and I'll get back to you as soon as I can. Remember, no question is too silly. As I said when we first discussed Dylan participating in this study, if there are any side-effects such as nausea, irritation to the skin, loss of appetite—anything like that—stop taking the medication instantly and call me.'

'OK.'

'You have the charts for the daily report of general health?' Jordanne confirmed.

'Yes.'

'Good. I'll need to see Dylan in one month's time with a new set of X-rays—do you have the request form?'

'Yes.'

'Have the X-rays like you did today, bring the daily reports, come here and see me. I'll need to do another blood test so perhaps next time we'll put a blindfold on him.'

Mrs Foster chuckled and nodded.

'And we'll take it from there.'

'Thanks, Doctor,' Dylan said, and his wife reiterated it.

'No. Thank *you*. Your participation in this study is greatly appreciated.' Jordanne checked his vital signs again, pleased that everything was back to normal. She helped Dylan to his feet while his wife handed him his crutches, and together they left.

Jordanne saw three more athletes who had agreed to take part in the study. The pharmaceutical company who was funding the research had also sent her X-rays and patient information on some of the athletes training at the IAS, whom the company sponsored.

Two of the athletes had been sent by the company. Jordanne had thoroughly read the information sent to her but when the candidates arrived, she gathered her own information.

Just as she was packing up for the day, there was another knock on her door. She looked up with a smile pasted on her face. The smile turned into a real one as Sally walked into her room and slumped down into the chair.

'It's Friday afternoon and I'm finally finished,' Sally said, and Jordanne laughed.

'I know exactly what you mean. Did Alex give you the details for Sunday night's dinner?'

'Yes.' Sally smiled. 'But I can't wait until Sunday, so spill the beans. What's going on between you and Alex?'

Jordanne hesitated for a moment. She didn't want to put Sally in a compromising position of keeping a secret from Jed because at the moment Jordanne definitely did *not* want her brother to know what was going on—*if anything*—between his little sister and his best friend. On the other hand, she could really use Sally's advice.

'I'm not really sure,' Jordanne said slowly.

Sally nodded. 'I remember that phase.' She grimaced. 'It'll pass. You've got to believe that.'

'Sally…' Jordanne reached for her friend's hand and held it. She took a deep breath. 'I feel a bit uncomfortable talking to you about this, just like you felt uncomfortable telling me what was going on between you and Jed.'

'I understand,' Sally said, and squeezed Jordanne's hand. 'Thank you for caring about my relationship with Jed.'

'No secrets,' Jordanne whispered. 'It's the philosophy my parents live by and I know Jed does, too.'

'Look, we don't have to go into details,' Sally reasoned. 'But, if I may, I'd like to offer some advice.'

'Go right ahead.'

'Take control. If you believe you and Alex should be together then go for it. As I said, take control, take a chance. I did.' Sally smiled at her friend and stood up. 'Now, how about…coffee and cake? I'd like to get your opinion on some of the wedding organising I'm doing.'

'I thought you were going to hire a professional wedding organiser?' Jordanne asked as she reached for her bag and keys.

'My mother's helping but this is something I want to do myself. I'm only going to get married once and I want it to be perfect.'

Jordanne nodded as she locked up her office and headed out with Sally, glad to have a distraction from her constant thoughts about Alex.

Saturday night's call was hectic. An eight-car pile-up on the highway leading into Canberra had brought several casualties with it. Accident and Emergency was chaotic and the ESS Theatres were constantly filled with one patient after the other.

Jordanne walked quickly down to Radiology to retrieve some X-rays Alex was eager to have.

'Hi, Jordanne,' Bethany Young, one of the senior radiographers greeted her. 'Talk about busy. I'm just putting the films you need through right now.' Bethany fed an X-ray into the machine and the two women waited for it to do its job. 'At least this machine hasn't broken down again. Tonight would not be a good night to be processing by hand!'

'Agreed,' Jordanne said, and leaned against the bench. She tried to stifle a yawn but wasn't successful.

'How many cups of coffee have you had tonight?' Bethany asked with a laugh.

'Far too many,' Jordanne replied.

Bethany gave her a close look. 'Things aren't going too well between you and Alex, huh?'

Jordanne was instantly alert. 'Our working relationship is just fine,' she said with what she hoped was firm clarity.

'Come off it. I don't buy the grapevine's rumour that you're just like brother and sister. I *know* your brother, remember? And I know Alex. We've all been friends for many years. Alex doesn't look upon you as sister material.'

Jordanne lowered her head and sighed a deep, heavy sigh. 'Please, don't—'

'My lips are sealed. I just like to see people happy in love rather than the alternative.'

'As you've known him for so long, do you have any advice?'

'Don't rush him,' Bethany said, and it was the last thing that Jordanne wanted to hear.

'Oh, I'm so confused,' she wailed.

'Here, then.' Bethany handed her a film. 'Focus on work for the next few hours, fall into bed through utter exhaustion and I'm sure the world will look a little more rosy tomorrow.'

Jordanne accepted the film. 'I hope you're right,' she said, before rushing out of Radiology and heading back towards theatres.

Jordanne couldn't but help follow Bethany's advice as they were in Theatre well into Sunday morning. Wearily, she crawled into bed and slept soundly for well over ten hours. By the time she woke, she had less than two hours to figure out her game plan, shower, dress and make it over to Alex's house for what she hoped would be the night to change his mind about her.

Beneath the hot spray, Jordanne tried to focus her thoughts. Most of the advice she'd received had been not to rush Alex. Indeed, from what she knew of him, he wasn't a man who appreciated being pushed into *any* situation, let alone a romantic one.

But it had been his decision, his breath, his lips that had brushed across hers last Tuesday. He'd admitted the attraction but that any relationship between them would be a mistake. She admired his concern about his friendship with Jed and it only made her love him all the more.

Jordanne also knew her brother. She was positive that once Jed found out how happy she and Alex were together, he would drop the over-protective big brother routine she'd dealt with for years and accept them as a couple.

'You're not the type of person to beat about the bush,' Jordanne told herself as she turned off the taps. 'Sally suggested going for it and...' she reached for a towel and looked at her reflection in the mirror '...that's exactly what you're going to do. The original plan was to bring Alex to his senses tonight, and after that kiss the other day you're going to take the chance.' She nodded firmly to herself as she wrapped up and walked to her bedroom.

So why did she still feel uncertain? Perhaps it was because she'd never done anything like this before in her life. There had never been so much at stake. She took some deep steadying breaths. It had to work. She had to show Alex how perfect they were for each other or else she'd... Tears blurred in her eyes at the thought of life without Alex by her side.

Jordanne looked at the dress she'd planned to wear. It wasn't at all suitable for the cool spring weather outside but she was prepared to freeze a little if it prompted Alex to warm her up.

The short red dress fitted her body like a glove and showed off her long, slender legs. Jordanne brushed her dark hair and arranged it around her shoulders. She took time with her make-up, ensuring she emphasised her eyes and mouth. She wore little jewellery and slipped her feet into a pair of sparkling red stilettos.

Twirling in front of the mirror, she smiled at her reflection. 'You can do this, Jordanne,' she told herself, and struck a sexy pose. 'Look out, Alex Page. I'm going to make you come to your senses tonight!'

Jordanne drove over to his house, only getting lost by one street, and parked on the road so as not to block the driveway. After she'd locked the car door, Jordanne pulled her warm coat firmly around her, tucking her hair in so it didn't wisp about in the wind. Calming her nerves, she walked to the front door and pressed the doorbell.

No one answered and for a fleeting moment Jordanne thought Alex had forgotten that they were going to their 'official dinner' together. The sound of the garage door opening caused her to turn. She heard the sound of a car's engine and watched as the Jaguar was driven slowly from its hiding place.

When the length of the car was visible to her, the garage door closed automatically. Jordanne stood, glued to the spot, her heart hammering wildly against her ribs. The car stopped and the driver's door opened.

Her eyes widened and her gaze never left Alex as he sauntered around the car and held open the passenger door. He was dressed in a black tuxedo as the restaurant was definitely five star. Her lips parted and she sucked in a breath.

'Care for a ride?' he asked, raising an eyebrow.

Jordanne couldn't speak. Instead, she nodded and carefully made her way down the path towards him. She made sure her calf-length coat was still closed as he handed her into the car. The coat rode up, displaying a certain amount of her leg.

At Alex's groan Jordanne looked up at him, only to see his gaze hungrily drinking in what she'd revealed. Pretending not to notice, she quickly covered her legs up and he shut the door. Again, she watched him as he came around the front of the car before he slid into the driver's seat. The way he moved, with such sure and purposeful strides, made her long to touch him. She clamped her hands into fists to stop them from fulfilling the action.

'Buckle up,' he said huskily. When Jordanne didn't move, he reached across her, his warm body pressing against hers momentarily as he pulled her seat belt down and clipped it in.

She breathed in the heady scent of his cologne and her eyelids fluttered closed. She'd known he was irresistible— but tonight he was obviously determined to drive her to distraction. How she fervently wished that the other three weren't coming along.

But, Jordanne recalled, without them she doubted Alex ever would have taken her out for her official dinner. As he set the car in motion, Jordanne tried to focus on her surroundings, tried to think of something to say that would immediately put them both at ease, but she couldn't think of anything except how close his thigh was to hers in the low-slung sports car.

He switched on some music as the streetlights overhead illuminated the windscreen.

'Chopin?' she asked after a moment.

'Yes.' He seemed surprised. 'Do you like it?'

'It's quite relaxing.'

'But you don't *really* like it.'

'I didn't say that,' she countered, enjoying the chance to actually have a conversation with him. Wasn't that what tonight was all about? Taking a chance?

'You've obviously listened to it before if you can name the composer only a few seconds into a piece.'

'Chopin is my father's favourite. Mozart is Jed's. Jared, my youngest brother, likes heavy metal.'

Alex smiled. 'What about Jordanne? What music do you like?'

'I like Strauss best. The "Blue Danube" waltz—it's so uplifting yet relaxing.'

Alex nodded. 'I can see that.' He pulled the Jaguar into a parking space just near the entrance to the restaurant. Jordanne placed her hand on the doorhandle. 'No, wait,' he urged. 'Allow me.'

Jordanne did as he suggested, watching hungrily his every move. When he opened the door, he held out his hand for her.

'Thank you.'

'My pleasure.' After he'd locked the car, Alex offered her his arm and Jordanne tentatively slipped her fingers around it. Being so close to him, feeling the warmth of his body radiate around her, mixing with the cool breeze, it sent goose-bumps cascading down her arms and back. As soon as they entered the foyer of the restaurant, Alex dropped his arm and reached around to help take her coat off.

Alex drew his breath in sharply as the coat revealed more and more of what Jordanne was wearing. The three, shoe-lace straps criss-crossed over her bare back, showing off her shoulder blades. From there, the material draped her body to perfection. Her dark hair cascaded around her shoulders, falling softly into place.

This is promising, she thought, and turned around to show him the front. His gaze travelled up her shapely legs to where the hem of the dress hung at mid-thigh. Jordanne held her breath as she waited for his eyes to meet her own. When they did, she read in his expression desire and hunger.

'Jordanne. Alex.' It was Sally who broke the moment and Alex spun around to face the rest of their dinner party.

'Jordanne—gorgeous dress,' Sally and Kirsten said as they came over to admire her.

'You look good, sis. All grown up.' Jed teased.

'Thanks, big brother.' She kissed his cheek. 'You don't look so bad yourself.' She motioned to his tux. 'Scrubs up nicely, doesn't he, Sally?'

Sally laughed but nodded emphatically and Jordanne started to relax a little. She risked a glance at Alex as they were all shown to their seats. He appeared cool, calm and collected yet she hoped he was still simmering with desire beneath it.

They chose their seats and Jordanne specifically sat next to Alex. Jed and Sally were opposite and Kirsten was at the head of the table. The camaraderie between the five of them was unrehearsed and enjoyable. The food was delicious and the service impeccable.

Just before dessert, the three women decided to head to the ladies room. Alex watched Jordanne rise gracefully from her chair, hungrily taking another look at that very sexy dress. His gaze quickly moved to look at Jed but thankfully his friend was ogling his fiancée.

They both watched as the women disappeared out of sight.

'I wish Jordanne wouldn't wear such a revealing dress,' Jed growled.

'Problem?' Alex asked, trying disguise the fact that he disagreed.

'Did you see the way the other men in the restaurant watched as she swished her way between the chairs?'

Alex frowned and cast a surreptitious glance around the room. He'd been so caught up in watching her for himself he hadn't stopped to notice that *other* men had found her attractive as well.

'Perhaps they were looking at Kirsten?' Alex offered. 'Or Sally? Your fiancée is a very attractive woman.'

'She certainly is, but everything about Sally's body language says "keep off" to any man who thinks he stands a chance. Except me, of course.'

'Of course,' Alex agreed with a smile.

'Jordanne, on the other hand, seems determined to flirt and flaunt herself tonight.'

'What makes you think that?'

'Her body language, combined with that dress, make a lethal combination as far as the lusting males in this room go. You don't have sisters, Alex, so take it from me. They're a handful.'

'Surely Jordanne doesn't need you as a watch dog?'

Jed thought about it for a second before glancing around the room once more. 'I've been a second father to her since the day she was born.'

'Hard habit to break?'

'Definitely. I'm very protective of my family, and my sisters in particular.' Jed raised his tone a notch. 'Second-best isn't good enough for them. I'll tell you this, though.' Jed tapped his index finger firmly on the table, punctuating every word he said. 'Any man who is *remotely* interested in dating *my* sister will have to go through *me* first.'

# CHAPTER SIX

JORDANNE noticed that Alex was rather quiet after she, Kirsten and Sally had returned from the ladies room. He was still outwardly happy but she sensed he was withdrawing—and mostly from her.

She glanced across at her brother. Had Jed said something to Alex? As it had only been the two of them who'd been left at the table, that had to be it. Jed was smiling at Sally before he leaned closer to kiss her.

Usually, witnessing such a scene would have caused Jordanne to sigh and get all misty-eyed, wishing it was her. At this moment in time, Jordanne was cross with her brother. Had Jed realised something was going on between herself and Alex? Had he put the hard word on Alex? She clenched her teeth. When would Jed learn that she could look after herself? She was thirty-four, for crying out loud.

'Jordanne?' Kirsten said quietly, and Jordanne turned from glaring at her brother to look at her friend. 'You all right?'

'Mmm. Fine,' Jordanne replied, making an effort to school her thoughts. After coffee, they sat around, talking. Jordanne used the opportunity to glean as much information about Alex as she could, asking him about his childhood and his brother.

He seemed a little hesitant at first and when he spoke he only provided the barest of details. 'Scott's three years younger than me. He and his wife, Amy, are both teachers, have two boys and are currently living and working in Boston.'

'Does it bother you?' Kirsten asked. 'You know that he's younger, and he has a wife and children.'

Jordanne watched as Alex clenched his jaw before forcing a smile. 'No. We're both very different people.'

His words sounded sincere but his body language told Jordanne there was more going on here than he wanted anyone to know about.

'No one can seriously put an age limit on when they plan to get married and start a family because it might not happen that way.'

'I agree,' Kirsten said. 'I have twin brothers—both younger than me. Wes is the elder by a whole ten minutes and Luke is the only one of us who's married and he's the youngest of the lot.'

'Isn't his wife due soon?' Sally asked.

'Yes. Within the next few weeks.'

'Family is so important,' Sally went on, and all of them nodded. Jordanne was happy to hear her friend talk like that, knowing that Sally had been through a tough time being an only child and not getting along with her parents until recently.

She turned to look at Alex who had relaxed a little. He glanced her way, a smile still playing about his lips. Their gazes held for a split second before he looked away, the smile disappearing. Something was definitely wrong.

'Alex, if it's all right with you, I'd like to get going soon,' she said as she gathered up her bag. 'We were in Theatre all night and left the hospital just before nine o'clock this morning,' she explained to the others.

'Was that the car pile-up?' Kirsten asked, and Alex nodded. 'I read about it in the morning paper. How are the patients?'

'Stable for now,' Alex replied. 'As neither Jordanne nor I have been paged, it's obviously stayed that way.' Alex rose from his seat and held Jordanne's chair for her as she followed suit.

'I think we all have a clinic first thing in the morning,' Jed said, and everyone nodded. 'Let's call it a night. It's been great.'

Everyone concurred.

'I forgot to mention,' Jed said after they'd collected their coats and were walking towards the car park, 'Sally and I are heading to Sydney next weekend to use the engagement present you gave us, Alex.'

'Good for you,' Alex said and shook his friend's hand heartily.

'We have to make the most of the weekends we're not on call,' Jed pointed out. 'After Sally's finished her Ph.D., we'll be splitting the workload more evenly.'

'You're going to be partners?' Jordanne squealed with delight. At Sally's nod, Jordanne stopped walking and threw her arms around her friend. 'Congratulations. That's the best news.'

'What are you talking about?' Jed asked, smiling at his sister and accepting her hug. 'I'd always planned to offer Sally a partnership in the practice.'

'Always?' Alex teased.

'Well…especially after I'd fallen in love with her,' Jed amended. 'Our engagement isn't just about romance, you know,' Jed said with a smile on his face. 'It's about being together in every way possible for the rest of our lives.'

Sally looked up at the man of her dreams. 'Well said.' She hugged him close.

The sound of a mobile phone ringing pierced the silence around them. Kirsten checked her handbag, Jed looked at his waistband.

'It's mine,' Alex said, and Jordanne groaned. He walked away from the small group to ensure a bit of privacy.

'I hope it's not another emergency,' Sally offered.

'You and me both,' Jordanne replied as she tried to stifle a yawn. 'I'm still tired from the last stint in Theatre.'

'Would you like us to wait?' Jed asked.

'No. You three get going. We'll probably need to go to the hospital anyway,' she said as Alex continued to talk into the phone. She kissed everyone goodnight. Alex waved as he listened intently to what was being said.

Jordanne pulled her coat more firmly around her as she waited for him to conclude the call.

'Sorry,' he said finally, and unlocked the car. They both climbed in. 'The elderly woman in the third car has died. Myocardial infarction. From what the nursing staff in ICU could tell it was natural. She simply slipped away in her sleep.'

'Do we need to go in?'

'No. They just wanted to notify us. I told them I'd let you know.'

'Thanks.'

Alex started the car and began to drive. Jordanne looked out of the window, aimlessly watching the lights, not caring where they were going.

'I hate losing a patient,' she said finally. 'It doesn't matter whether they've just come into A and E or whether I've been seeing them for quite some time. I still hate it.'

'I know what you mean,' he replied. The melancholy silence returned but neither of them seemed too troubled by it. Fifteen minutes later, Jordanne started to focus on the surroundings outside her window.

'Where are we?' she asked as Alex steered the Jag up a hill.

'There's something I want to show you.'

Jordanne was thrilled and her attitude lifted at the anticipation of sharing a new experience with Alex. The road was fairly winding now with no street lighting. When they were almost at the top Alex dimmed the headlights on the car and continued slowly, manoeuvring the car into a parking area.

'What is this place?' Jordanne asked.

'Mt Stromlo Observatory.'

'Why?'

He shrugged as he switched off the engine and turned to look at her. 'I like coming here, especially when I feel a little down. When a patient's died, when things aren't going right.'

'We're hardly dressed for star-gazing,' Jordanne told him as he undid her seat belt and came around to open her door.

'The stars don't care what you wear,' he whispered close to her ear. He led her across the car park to one of the domes that housed a telescope. He knocked twice on the door and waited.

Slowly the door opened and an elderly man poked his head around. 'Alex,' he said with a smile, and opened the door wider. 'And who is this lovely lady?'

'Harris Goldfinch, meet my colleague, Jordanne McElroy.'

Jordanne shook hands with the man, who sported the bushiest grey moustache that she'd ever seen.

'Any relation to Jed McElroy?' he asked.

'He's my brother,' Jordanne offered as they were shown inside. 'It's rather cool in here,' she stated.

'We need to keep the room close to the outside temperature so the mirrors can be used straight away. So, where have you two been tonight?' Harris's question was rather leading and he wiggled his bushy eyebrows up and down for emphasis.

'Just to dinner,' Alex replied, but didn't say anything more. 'No tours tonight?' he asked.

'I haven't been notified of a tour. Some nights we're packed and others we're not. It's a bit cloudy tonight but just before you knocked I was getting a good view. Come,' he said to Jordanne and held out his hand. 'Take a look.'

Jordanne felt a little uncomfortable climbing up the few steps in her stilettos but there wasn't anything she could do about it. The self-consciousness she felt over her appearance soon disappeared as she looked through the telescope at the bright shimmering stars.

'Wow!' she gasped in wonderment. 'It's incredible.'

Alex had a turn and after they'd been there for almost an hour he suggested they'd better get going. They said goodbye to Harris who resumed his work, gazing out into the beautiful universe above.

'Thank you,' Jordanne said as they walked towards the Jaguar.

'I knew you'd like it.'

'I'm amazed you shared it with me,' Jordanne said as she leaned against his car and looked up at the sky. Alex stood beside her.

'Why?' The word was spoken softly and Jordanne glanced at him briefly.

'I'm not complaining,' she clarified. 'It's…majestic out here but almost from the moment I started working with you you've been trying to keep your distance. Not only physically but emotionally.' Jordanne looked back up to the night sky. 'I know Jed said something to you tonight and it made you guarded. I realise you're concerned about your friendship with him and I admire that, but you can't keep denying the attraction we both feel.'

Jordanne returned her gaze to meet his. He was watching her intently. 'Life's too short, Alex.'

Without breaking eye contact, Alex took a few steps around to stand in front of her. 'It is.' He was silent, as

though warring with his feelings once more. 'I'm not worried about my friendship with Jed,' he confessed, and
Jordanne was surprised.

'But I thought you were?'

'Perhaps I was…concerned, but I know Jed would only
want what's best for you.'

'And that's *you*,' Jordanne said. She couldn't help it. She
wanted Alex to know that her feelings for him weren't run-
of-the-mill.

'That's still to be debated.'

Jordanne shook her head. 'Alex…I *want* to be with you.
I like hearing the sound of your voice. I like watching the
way you walk. I like working with you. Intellectually and
emotionally we're a perfect match.'

'I'll end up hurting you, Jordanne,' he confessed, his
tone laced with desire and regret. 'When that happens, I'll
not only have Jed angry with me but your other brothers
as well—*and* most probably your sister, too.'

'What if you *don't* hurt me? What if we fall in love and
live happily ever after?' she pressed gently, hoping she
didn't scare him off.

'You're deluding yourself,' he said softly as he gazed
deeply into her eyes. Her heart hammered wildly against
her ribs and she was positive he could hear it. They were
standing toe to toe now and Alex slowly raised his hands
to her chest.

His fingers worked the buttons on her coat, undoing each
one carefully. 'Jordanne,' he whispered as he slowly shook
his head, 'I'm a selfish man.' He stopped as he opened the
coat and looked at her.

'How can you say that? I know you're not,' she urged.

'If I don't hold you in my arms tonight, if I don't kiss
you the way I've been dreaming about for the past month,
if I pass up this opportunity…I'll regret it.'

'Then don't pass it up.'

He slid his hands gently around her waist and gathered her closer to him. Jordanne felt the warm pressure of his body against hers and the breath whooshed out of her in a rush.

'I'm sorry, Jordanne,' he whispered before his lips claimed hers in an electrifying kiss.

All the emotions Jordanne had been carefully holding onto poured over her in excitement. She wound her arms about his neck, ensuring he didn't pull away too suddenly.

The heady scent of his cologne weaved its way through her senses, causing her to become even more addicted to him than before. Her knees started to give way but Alex held her up, urging her closer to his body. His hands were warm on her bare back, the softness of his touch causing a spread of fireworks to explode within her.

Jordanne threaded her fingers through his hair one last time before sliding the palms of her hands down his neck and shoulders. They travelled further south, her fingertips delighting in the firm muscled torso beneath his white dress shirt.

Gently she edged her hands beneath his arms and around to his back. As she did so, his own hands slipped lower. Jordanne lightly ran her fingernails down the centre of his back, again marvelling at how incredible he felt beneath her touch.

'Mmm,' he groaned, and deepened the kiss even further. For a split second she was conscious of the real effect she had on him and was amazed at his previous self-control. She was ecstatic that it was finally shattered.

A moment or two later, Alex pulled his mouth from hers. 'Please, don't wear this dress in public again,' he ground out, his tone desire-filled. 'It causes way too much of a stir. I wanted to fight every other man who looked at you.'

Jordanne laughed softly. 'My hero,' she said, and looked into his deep blue eyes, drowning instantly. 'I promise to only wear this dress for you.'

'You're one incredibly sexy and beautiful woman, Jordanne McElroy.' Alex lowered his head and kissed her again. 'I can't get enough of you.'

'The feeling is quite mutual. I knew from the instant I threw my arms around you after you'd rescued Joel that there was something between us.'

'Chemistry.'

Jordanne glanced up at the stars above them. She shook her head. 'Fate.'

They were silent for a while, and even though his arms were still around her Jordanne sensed his emotional withdrawal from her.

'I'd better get you back to your car,' he said finally, and eased away. Jordanne gathered her coat around her, feeling bereft and cold without the warmth of Alex's body against her own.

They drove down Mt Stromlo and back to civilisation, the streetlights once again illuminating them as the car purred quietly through the suburbs. Alex had rummaged through his CD collection in the car but hadn't found any Strauss.

'It doesn't matter,' Jordanne said, keeping her tone light. 'I don't mind what we listen to.' She was trying to figure out what had happened to cause him to withdraw. Had she said something wrong?

He must have picked up on her tone because he groaned in exasperation. 'Ah-h, Jordanne. You give so much of yourself so freely. You're going to have to be careful.'

'Why?' He didn't answer. 'Besides, I'm a big girl,' she reminded him with a sexy smile.

'I'd noticed.' He gave her a brief glance that rocketed

her senses once more. At the edge of his driveway he pressed the remote control for the garage door, and after it had opened he drove the Jag in.

Switching off the engine, he turned to face her. 'Coffee?'

Jordanne smiled at him. 'Unfortunately, I think I'd better get home and go to sleep. My boss doesn't like to run late on his clinics.'

'He's a tyrant, is he?' Alex asked with a grin.

'The worst.' Jordanne rolled her eyes mockingly, the teasing nature disappearing immediately as Alex leaned in closer before kissing her softly. Jordanne's eyelids fluttered closed as her lips parted, willingly surrendering to the masterful manoeuvring of his mouth on hers.

'Call in sick,' he murmured, his breathing as ragged as her own.

Jordanne cradled his face in her hands. She kissed him briefly before taking a deep breath. 'So tempting.' She bit her lower lip. 'But then you'd have to call in sick, too, and I fear it may look just a *little* bit conspicuous.'

Alex sat back and nodded. 'You're right.' He opened the door, asking her to wait again. Jordanne undid her seat belt whilst Alex walked around the car. The door beside her opened and once more he offered her his hand to help her out.

Jordanne swung one leg out and then the other, revealing a good amount of sculptured calves and thighs. Alex helped her up, being careful not to knock her head against the car.

He pulled her into his arms and plundered her mouth. This kiss was hot and hungry, his hands were everywhere, as were Jordanne's. She matched the force of his kiss equally, allowing her own hunger for him to come to the fore.

Eventually, Alex broke free and trailed passionate kisses down Jordanne's neck, across her shoulder and upper arm before he dipped slightly lower towards the valley between her breasts. Jordanne tipped her head back, revelling in his touch. This was where she belonged—in Alex's arms.

'You smell so good,' he ground out as the kisses started working their way up towards her other shoulder. 'You taste so good.'

'Mmm,' Jordanne murmured as she rolled her head to the other side, allowing him access.

Finally his lips found her mouth again and he plunged his fingers into her flowing hair, holding her head firmly in place. Not only did she taste and smell good, Alex had the strangest feeling that she was also becoming addictive.

With what amounted to superhuman effort, he pulled back and looked down into Jordanne's upturned face. He breathed out slowly as she opened her eyes. Taking a step back from her, he shoved his hands into his pockets. 'I'll walk you to your car,' he said, his breathing still ragged. It gave him immense satisfaction, though, to see that Jordanne needed a few moments to convince her legs to support her. She was correct in one respect—it *did* feel so right to be in each other's arms.

Alex placed one hand around her waist for support as they walked towards the road, drawing in another deep breath, only to have his senses assaulted by that incredible perfume she wore.

He groaned and tightened his grip around her waist. Jordanne turned to look at him and laughed.

'I know how you feel,' she said softly.

Against her car, Alex took her in his arms and kissed her goodnight. When she opened the driver's door, Alex kissed her goodnight. When she was seated with her seat belt fastened and the window down, Alex kissed her goodnight.

'There is one thing,' he said as she put her key in the ignition. When she turned her face to look expectantly up at him, Alex was once more struck by her beauty. Her hair, her eyes, her neck, her lips…

'Yes?' she prompted, and he realised he was staring.

Alex cleared his throat. 'I'd rather be the one to tell Jed about what happened tonight, if you don't mind.'

Jordanne looked down at the steering-wheel. 'When will that be?' she asked, before glancing back up at him.

'Soon,' he promised, and kissed her again. 'Jordanne McElroy, you have a way of getting under a man's skin and driving him to distraction.'

Jordanne laughed. 'I hope that's a *good* thing?'

'My resolve this evening was to keep you at arm's length and if you tried anything I was going to politely tell you that there could never be anything more than friendship between us.'

Jordanne tilted her head to one side and looked at him in amazement. 'Even after that brief kiss the other day, you were still going to say no?'

He nodded and kissed her again.

'So what made you change your mind?'

'My resolve was whisked away with the wind the instant I saw you standing at my front door.'

'Before you saw the dress?'

'The dress…' Alex whistled. 'No, the dress knocked me for six.' Alex leaned in through the open window and kissed her again. 'You've knocked me for six,' he amended, 'and I can't seem to keep my hands or my lips off you.'

'Do you hear me complaining?'

Alex grimaced. 'Right now, though, I'm starting to lose all feeling in my toes and fingers due to the iciness of that wind.' Alex kissed her once more. It was a slow and arousing kiss, filled with promise. 'Drive safely,' he whispered, and cleared his throat. 'See you in the morning.'

'Sweet dreams,' she told him, before beckoning him closer for just one more tiny kiss before she started the engine.

Alex watched her drive away before slowly making his way inside the house. He was a first class cad for what he'd just done to her. He didn't need to be told that Jordanne McElroy was a woman who deserved marriage and a family and there was no way he could ever provide her with both.

On the other hand, whenever she was near, he was unable to stop the power she wielded over him. She was hypnotic, like a drug coursing through his blood, lifting him up to a place so high he never wanted to come down.

Alex crossed to the mirror in the bathroom and looked at his reflection with disgust. 'Break it off tomorrow,' he told himself sternly. 'Before you *really* break her heart.'

Jordanne slept better that night than she had during the week. They were a couple, she told herself the next morning as she dressed for work. Jordanne McElroy and Alex Page were dating.

Whenever she'd started dating a man seriously in the past, Jordanne would be on the phone to her mother and her sister Jasmine, as well as Kirsten and Sally, discussing him in a lot of detail.

This time, however, it felt nice to share the knowledge with only Alex. Perhaps it was because she already knew she was in love with him so she wasn't that keen to dissect every move he made with her family and friends.

'Patience,' she told her reflection as she finished putting on her make-up. She reminded herself of the way he'd withdrawn a few times last night and he'd openly confessed that he wasn't really worried about Jed's approval. Her intuition told her that something else was wrong, and if she didn't proceed with caution she would run the risk of losing him altogether.

When she finally arrived at the hospital, Jordanne rushed to the ward just in time for the start of the ward round. They'd been doing roadwork, and the detour had almost made her late, leaving her no opportunity to say a proper good morning to Alex.

As the group of consultants, registrars, interns, nursing staff, physiotherapists, occupational therapists and the social worker toured the ward, checking and discussing patients, Jordanne was acutely aware of Alex's presence. For the most part he stood opposite her and only once did their gazes meet.

She felt very conscious of all the other people and could have sworn they could read in her face the truth of her new relationship with the director of the department. Taking a breath and telling herself not to be so paranoid, Jordanne forced herself to concentrate on the rest of the round.

When they were finally finished, Jordanne stopped by to check on Louise Kellerman. It was almost a blessing to slip into the private room, away from the hustle and bustle of the ward. Louise was sitting up in bed, looking better.

'Ready for breakfast?' Jordanne asked as Alex came in behind her and crossed to the foot of Louise's bed. Her heart pounded wildly against her ribs as she glanced across at him, but he was engrossed in the patient chart.

'Everything seems to be healing nicely,' he stated, looking directly at Louise who nodded.

'How's the pain?' Jordanne asked.

'OK. The nursing staff have reduced the number of tablets I've been taking.'

'And you're coping fine with that?' Alex asked.

'Yes,' Louise answered proudly. The door to her room opened again and Dean, the social worker, came in.

'Sorry,' he apologised quickly, his colour rising as he looked at Jordanne and Alex as though he'd been caught with his hand in the cookie jar. His gaze settled on Louise, who smiled shyly at him.

Hello, Jordanne thought. What's going on here? 'Come on in, Dean. We'll be out of here in a few more seconds. Stay and keep Louise company.'

'How's everything going from your perspective?' Alex asked Dean.

'Great. Emotionally, Louise is making an uncomplicated recovery.'

'Dean organised for my bed to be wheeled outside yesterday,' Louise told them. 'Although it was cold, it was great to be out in the fresh air again.'

'Good.' Jordanne nodded and looked from patient to social worker, intercepting a glance that said it all. It seemed as though Louise's track record with men was changing for the better. If there was a romantic interest between the two of them, it was no wonder her recovery had suddenly picked up. She only hoped Dean had the sense to transfer Louise's management to another social worker. 'Finished, Alex? We'd better get to clinic.'

He looked up and frowned at her. He made a note on Louise's chart before they said their goodbyes.

'What's the rush?' he asked her quietly after the door had shut behind them. Before Jordanne could answer, Dean came out again.

'Um…I wanted to ask your permission about something,' he said, and took a deep breath. 'Louise has a cat,' he began.

'A cat,' Alex repeated.

'I was wondering if I could bring it up for her to see it. She's really missing it.'

Alex frowned again and opened his mouth to comment but the social worker quickly rushed on.

'I won't bring it inside the hospital. If Louise's bed is outside, I can take the cat to her.'

Alex looked at Jordanne as if to say, Do you believe this?

'I don't think—' he began, but Jordanne placed her hand on his arm, stopping him.

'She *was* very distressed about the cat last week,' she said. 'If this happens, there are going to be some strict rules. She would only be able to pat him. He can't go on the bed or we risk infection, especially with the fixator pin sites. I want her hands and her face, if she insists on kissing him which she probably will, disinfected before she re-enters the ward. What do you think, Alex?'

He looked down at her hand, which was still resting on his arm, and she quickly removed it. 'I'll think about it and let you know,' he told Dean, before turning on his heel and stalking out of the ward.

'I'll try and bring him around,' Jordanne told Dean.

'Thanks…and don't say anything to Louise. I don't want to get her hopes up.'

'Fair enough,' Jordanne replied with a smile. 'Dean? I hope you don't think I'm out of line here but I did notice just now the way you and Louise seem to…well…feel about each other.'

'Oh?' The social worker blushed beetroot red.

'I just wanted to know if you'd planned on transferring her care to someone else?'

'Ah. Good point. Yes. I see. Yes. I'll look into that today but if you still wouldn't mind asking Alex about the cat?'

'Sure. No problem, but I'd better get to clinic immediately or I'll never get Alex back into a good mood.'

'You can do it, Jordanne,' Dean replied. 'If anyone can, you can.'

It was Jordanne's turn to frown. 'What do you mean by that?' she asked cautiously.

'Your family connection. I know you think of each other as brother and sister. So go to it, sis. Change his mind.'

Jordanne smiled with relief and hurried from the ward, heading for her office. There was no time to discuss anything with Alex before clinic, but when she entered her office her phone was ringing.

'Dr McElroy,' she answered.

'Hi, Jordanne. It's Sky, from the IAS library.'

'What's up?'

'I've had some more X-rays delivered here for you. They won't fit in your pigeonhole and I didn't know if they were urgent. Do you want me to hold onto them until your session here tomorrow or send them to the hospital?'

'Put them in the courier that goes between the hospital and the IAS. Mark them urgent and that way I should get them this afternoon.'

'Will do,' Sky said.

'Thanks,' Jordanne said, before disconnecting the call. Obviously the pharmaceutical company had found another candidate for her study. Hopefully it would be the last, otherwise she'd have too many patients to interview and track. She quickly checked with Alex's secretary on the way to clinic and made an appointment to see Alex that afternoon to discuss the research study further.

'How was your weekend?' Trudy Elliot asked as Jordanne came into the clinic.

Jordanne thought for a moment and hid the smile that threatened to spread across her face. 'Hectic on Saturday night.'

'That's right, you and Alex were on call. Terrible accident.' She shook her head.

'How was yours?'

'Relaxing.'

'I don't want to know,' Jordanne said mockingly.

'Clinic,' Alex's deep voice boomed from behind them, and Jordanne jumped.

'You just like scaring me, don't you?' she asked rhetorically, and smiled up at him before heading to her consulting room. Seeing a constant flow of patients, one after the other, Jordanne had little time to think about Alex and his strange behaviour.

When clinic finally finished she went to the cafeteria, hoping there was some food left as it was the end of the lunchtime rush. The staff made her up a salad sandwich and she ate it as she walked to her office.

Slumping down into the chair, she removed her stethoscope and took another bite of her sandwich. Looking at her desk, she noticed a packet of X-rays sitting on top of her paperwork.

'Thank you, Sky,' she mumbled as she stuffed the last of her sandwich into her mouth and reached for the X-rays. She took them out of the packet and held them up to the light. She blinked and frowned before getting up to switch on the X-ray viewing box. She hooked the films up and stared at the fracture before her. Her gaze jumped to the name of the patient.

'Ethan Hoe?' she said out loud. 'It can't be.' Jordanne looked at the fracture again. 'Something's wrong here.'

# CHAPTER SEVEN

JORDANNE stormed up the corridor to Alex's office. She tucked the two sets of X-rays under her arm, knocked on his door and went in without waiting for his reply.

'Sorry I'm late,' she told him. 'I had to rush over to the IAS to pick something up.' Jordanne headed straight for his viewing box. 'Take a look at these.' She hooked one of the X-rays with the name 'Ethan Hoe' on it and beside it she hooked up one of Dylan Foster's.

Alex looked at them both and frowned. 'They're identical.'

'I know. Dylan had these views taken on Friday, specifically for the research study. I requested them myself.'

'How did this happen? Did the radiographer put the wrong name on the X-ray?'

'That's what I thought, but surely once they discovered their mistake the copied films should have been destroyed. After all, there are Dylan's X-rays sitting right next to it.'

'Is it just this one?'

'No, it's the entire set.'

Alex glanced at her. 'Obviously someone on the clerical staff hasn't destroyed them.'

'But why were they sent to me? I thought they were from the pharmaceutical company but now I'm not so sure.'

'Who's the referring doctor?'

They both peered at the films. 'Dr J. Scelero. Never heard of him,' Alex said.

'Where are the reports?' Jordanne rummaged through both packets for the reports. 'All right,' she said when she had them side by side. 'Here's the one I requested for Dylan.' She looked at the one for Ethan. 'That's impossible.'

'What?' Alex asked as he looked from the films to her.

'The reports have different letterheads.'

Alex took the reports she was holding side by side. 'The *same* X-rays from two different radiographer companies?' He looked back to the X-rays again. 'The date on this X-ray is from six months ago.' He shook his head. 'There's been a *big* mix-up here.'

He crossed to his desk and Jordanne followed, pulling up a chair to sit next to him. 'Let me take some notes. Dr J. Scelero,' he said as he wrote it down. 'What's the name of the radiologist who signed Ethan's report?'

They compiled a list and checked the numbers in the phone book. 'You ring the firm you sent Dylan to and just check that they didn't send his films anywhere else,' Alex suggested as he picked up the phone.

'I'll also ring the pharmaceutical company just to make sure the films weren't sent from them.'

'Good.'

Jordanne returned to her office and made the calls. She spoke with the radiologist who had reported on Dylan's films, asking him leading questions as she didn't want him to know what was going on. When she called the pharmaceutical company, she was blocked at every turn when she requested to speak to one of the organisers of the grant. So she left a message with the secretary, asking her to check whether some X-rays had been forwarded to her at the IAS.

'Haven't you received them?' the secretary asked. 'I sent them out by a courier earlier today.'

'Oh, so they *did* come from your company.'

'Yes. Is there a problem?'

Jordanne didn't like the other woman's patronising tone so decided to be vague. 'No. I wasn't sure who'd sent them as the IAS forwarded them to the hospital. Thanks for your help.'

Before the secretary could say another word, Jordanne hung up. She almost ran up the corridor back to Alex's office. He was just concluding a call.

'Anything?' he asked when he saw her.

'The company *did* send them.'

'How did they get hold of Dylan Foster's X-rays with someone else's name on them?'

Jordanne shrugged. 'Did Dr J. Scelero check out?'

'Yes, he's a GP in the southern suburbs, but he's never seen an Ethan Hoe and sends his patients to a different X-ray place when they require films. I also called the other firm of radiographers and they don't have a member of staff by this name,' Alex said as he pointed to Ethan's report.

'*Is* there an athlete called Ethan Hoe?' Jordanne wondered out loud.

'Why don't you ring the IAS and find out?' Alex suggested, holding the telephone receiver out to her.

A few moments later, Jordanne replaced the receiver. 'Sky, the librarian out at the IAS, knows everyone and everything about that place. Yes, there is an athlete called Ethan Hoe. He's in track and field, his specialty being the triple jump.'

Alex rubbed his chin with his thumb and forefinger as he thought. 'Why would the company send us these X-rays?' He glanced across the room at the viewing box where the films in question were still illuminated. 'How many other patients have they sent you?'

'Seven, and this makes eight.'

'Have you interviewed the others?'

'Yes, I did the last two on Friday.'

'Set up a meeting with Ethan Hoe as soon as you can. Get all the names of the other athletes the company have sent you. We need to take a closer look at them.'

'I'll arrange to meet with the infamous Mr Hoe tomorrow morning.' Jordanne smiled down at him, her eyes twinkling with excitement.

'You be careful,' he warned.

'Yes, boss,' she replied primly, her gaze teasing him.

Alex looked at her and frowned.

'What?' She spread her arms wide, feigning innocence.

'You!'

Jordanne leaned against his desk, adopting a sexy pose. 'What *about* me?'

Alex's gaze crossed to his closed office door before returning to Jordanne, his frown deepening. 'No flirting during business hours,' he growled.

Jordanne inclined her head to one side. 'Didn't you sleep well last night?'

'The question you should be asking is did I sleep at all?'

'Ooh, I didn't realise I was *that* irresistible.'

'Jordanne!' He stood, putting some distance between them. 'Around the hospital we have to be—'

'Brother and sister?' she cooed at him.

'Professional,' he amended.

Jordanne grimaced. 'I like my answer better.'

'Stop it.'

'Oh, Alex, calm down.' She crossed to his side. 'What have I done this morning that's been so terrible? You ignored me throughout ward round and frightened the life out of me in clinic.'

'What did you do?' he asked disbelievingly. 'I'll tell you. You smell incredible. You look fantastic. I keep remembering the way you felt in my arms and how delicious you tasted. You're driving me insane.' Alex raked an unsteady hand through his hair.

'Oh, is that all?' she replied, attempting to be blasé. His words had touched her so deeply, her heart turned over with love for him. 'I *had* hoped I'd been driving you insane since we started working together, not just since last night.'

Alex looked down into her face but made no move to touch her. 'The attraction I feel for you is *worse* than it was before last night. The red top you're wearing now reminds me of that amazing dress. When I look at your hair in that ridiculous bun, all I want to do is pull the pins out and run my fingers through those long, dark locks. And when I look into your eyes...' Alex let his sentence trail off as he did just that.

Jordanne felt the air whoosh out and her heart start its erratic rhythm. Neither of them moved. Alex's gaze penetrated deep down within her, causing her senses to swirl with the desire she saw in those hypnotic blue eyes of his.

'Can't you hear my heart beating?' she whispered in a rush. 'It seems so loud—always does when you're near.'

Alex clenched his hands into fists at his sides, desperately trying to control himself.

'I'm sorry,' she said as she quickly closed the gap between them before pressing her mouth firmly against his.

Alex stayed motionless for a split second before his arms came around her body, hauling her closer to him. The intensity of the kiss was equally matched, their hunger for each other growing at an alarming rate with each passing second.

Jordanne felt on fire, such was the effect Alex had on her. 'I'm burning up,' she groaned against his mouth as his lips moved over her neck.

The buzzing of the intercom on his desk made them both spring apart with the speed of a rope recoiling after a bungee jump. They stared at each other, the desire still lighting their eyes, their breathing still uneven.

Alex stalked over to his desk and punched a button. 'Yes.'

'You have five minutes until your next meeting,' his secretary's voice came through the intercom.

'Thank you.' He turned to face Jordanne slowly and for an instant she wasn't at all sure what he would do or say. She held her breath.

'Which part of the words ''professional relationship'' don't you understand?' he asked with a lopsided grin.

Jordanne smiled back. 'The same part *you* obviously don't understand,' she countered. They stayed where they were—almost on opposite sides of his office. 'You'd better get ready for your meeting.'

'It's with Jed,' he told her.

'I see. So you're going to tell him about us. Do you want me to be there, too?'

'No. As I said last night, I'd rather do it. You know, man to man.'

Jordanne nodded, still smiling, before turning to take the X-rays from the viewing machine. 'Good luck, then. Right now I need to reorganise my research plan for tomorrow morning.'

'We'll have a meeting after the operating list is finished tomorrow evening,' he told her as he marked it down in his diary.

'Sure.' Jordanne tucked the X-rays under her arm and headed for the door.

'Jordanne?'

She stopped when he called her name and turned slowly to look at him.

'Dinner tonight?' His tone held regret and she noticed a

sadness in his eyes. She wished she knew what he was thinking.

'Sounds good. Are you on the menu?'

'Jordanne!' His gaze flashed with a spark of desire at her teasing. 'No, I'm not. We need to…talk.'

Jordanne gulped but kept her tone light. 'You're the boss, *boss*. Seven o'clock, your place. I'll bring dessert.' With that she left his office and walked down the corridor, ignoring the nagging feeling that things weren't as right as she thought they'd be.


'So what did you want to discuss so urgently?' Jed asked after he'd closed the door to his consulting room.

Alex sat down in the chair opposite Jed but then stood to pace the room. He stopped and looked across at his friend, frowning intently.

'I have something to tell you but I have no idea how you're going to react.'

'Spit it out, Page.'

Alex took a deep breath. 'I kissed Jordanne last night.'

Jed was silent for a moment and Alex clenched his jaw tightly, waiting for his friend to respond.

'So *that's* why she wore that dress.' Jed nodded. 'She's interested in you.'

'Yes.'

'And…you're interested in her?'

Alex raked a hand through his hair and crossed to the chair he'd vacated. 'She's an incredible woman,' he said, after sitting down.

'That she is.' Jed's tone held a warning note. 'But you haven't answered the question.'

Alex took a deep breath and momentarily closed his eyes. 'Yes.' His eyes snapped open. 'I'm interested in her.' He stood again to pace the room. 'I don't know, Jed. She drives me insane.' He shook his head. 'One minute she's looking at me with those incredible eyes, reaching deep down into my soul, and the next she's teasing, making me laugh. It all seems to have happened so quickly, and believe me...' he held his hands outward, palms up '...I've tried to ignore it as well as stop it.'

'But you can't,' Jed stated.

'I can't.' Alex agreed, rubbing his fingers across his forehead.

'So what are you going to do about it?'

'There's only one thing I can do. Call it off.'

'What?'

'I'm having dinner with her tonight. I'm going to tell her it was a mistake and that we shouldn't pursue the attraction.'

'Why? If you really feel this tied up in knots about Jordanne, then you owe it to yourself *and* to her to find out where it's going to lead you. Jordanne isn't a woman to make a commitment lightly. When she does, it will be for ever.'

'That's what I'm afraid of. That's why I *need* to break it off. Now!'

'Why? Because you're afraid of marriage again? I thought you were over that?'

'It's not the commitment factor that I have a problem with.'

'Then what is it?'

Alex raked both hands through his hair. 'I knew I shouldn't have kissed her,' he mumbled more to himself than to Jed. He looked his friend squarely in the eye. 'Do you know why my marriage broke up?'

Jed shook his head. 'You never told me.'

'It was because we couldn't have children.' The words were spoken softly and still held a hint of longing. Alex fought the pain saying those words had evoked. His parents, his brother and now his friend knew. It might have been seventeen years since he'd signed the divorce papers but the raw emotion he'd felt back then hadn't diminished over time—it had just been pushed aside.

Both men were silent, the ticking of the clock the only sound in the room. Jed slowly exhaled. 'Tough break.'

'Now, I can tell, without even asking, that Jordanne would want children.'

Jed nodded.

'That's why I have to break it off. I can't do that to her. It isn't fair.'

'I take it she doesn't know.'

'Of course she doesn't. I only really kissed her for the first time last night. Until then I'd been desperately trying to keep my distance, but you know your sister.'

'Oh, yeah. Once she gets an idea in her head, it's virtually impossible to dislodge it.'

'I can't risk hurting her, Jed.'

'She means *that* much to you?'

'You—her. Both of you. If I hurt Jordanne, I risk our friendship as well. It's the reason I wanted to be up-front with you.'

'Why don't you tell her what you told me and let her make her own decision?'

'Don't you think it's a bit early in the relationship to start bringing up marriage and children? What if we find we're not compatible?'

'Just give the two of you a bit of time,' Jed encouraged.

'But what if it doesn't work out? I don't want to hurt her.'

'That's the risk we all take.'

That night, Alex decided to put all of his concerns aside and simply enjoy being with Jordanne, which was quite easy to do as she was very good company. She didn't ask about his meeting with Jed and he didn't offer any details. It was as though both of them had called a truce and were happy being in each other's company.

They ate together on Tuesday night as well but this time at Jordanne's house.

'That operating session wasn't too bad,' Jordanne commented as she finished making a beef stir-fry. Alex sat on a bar stool at the bench, watching her intently.

He sipped his wine. 'At least we didn't go overtime. I hate hospital red tape and politics. Whatever happened to care for the patients being of primary concern? Instead, it's get them fixed and get them out of the hospital as soon as possible.'

'Economics,' Jordanne agreed with a nod. 'This is ready so let's eat.'

'Smells delicious,' he murmured as she walked past him, carrying the food. He nibbled at her neck.

'Stop it.' She laughed. 'You'll make me drop dinner and I don't fancy eating off the floor.'

Alex held her chair for her and Jordanne kissed him. 'Thank you.'

'So, what happened today with Ethan Hoe,' he asked as he sat down and expertly used the chopsticks to lift a snow pea into his mouth.

'Nothing out of the ordinary, but all of the answers he gave to my questions…well, it *appeared* as though he was ready for them.'

'He'd anticipated them?'

'Yes. He didn't hesitate or need to think about things.'

'Most patients do,' Alex said.

'Especially when the injury was supposed to have occurred six months ago.'

'Did anyone receive a list of your questions? The pharmaceutical company? The coaches?'

'No.' Jordanne shook her head and frowned. 'I've brought home all the files of the athletes the company have recommended for the study so perhaps we can find some clues as to what's going on here. Oh, I've also asked Sky to let me know as soon as the blood test results for Ethan Hoe arrive. They should be sent to the IAS, not the hospital.'

Alex nodded, his mouth full. 'Good. This tastes great,' he praised after he'd swallowed. 'You're a good cook, Jordanne McElroy.'

'Thank you, Dr Page.' She leaned over and gave him a kiss. 'Feel free to compliment me any time.'

'I might just do that,' he murmured against her lips before he kissed her again. After a few more moments he pulled back and cleared his throat. Taking a sip of his wine, he looked at her. 'Back to business. Louise Kellerman's doing extremely well.'

'I think it's all the…*help*, for want of a better word, that she's been receiving from Dean.'

'The ward social worker?'

Jordanne sighed and shook her head. 'Are all men blind?'

'I thought she'd been in better spirits because we'd allowed her to see her cat.'

Jordanne laughed. 'But was it seeing the cat or the fact that Dean had organised the whole thing?'

Alex shook his head in bemusement. 'Regardless of whatever it is that's making her happy, it's working. I hope Dean has transferred her care if he has romantic feelings for her.'

'I spoke to him about that yesterday morning. He said he'd look into it.'

'Good. I've had good reports from the physio and the occupational therapist. The set of X-rays she had taken today showed everything to be healing well without further complications. The pin sites for the external fixator have cleared up, and with the bruising now almost non-existent she'll be up and roller-blading again in no time.'

'Don't let Louise hear you say that. She doesn't want to have anything to do with those ''contraptions'', as she calls them, ever again.'

Alex laughed and Jordanne enjoyed the way the sound reverberated throughout her being, bringing a smile to her own face. She loved spending time with him, and the more they were together, the more Jordanne's love for him increased.

After dinner, Alex prepared the dessert while Jordanne set out the documentation concerning the athletes on the coffee-table in the lounge room.

'Here you go,' he said as he handed her a bowl.

'Wow. Ice cream. When you provide dessert, Alex, you don't hold back a thing.'

'It's boysenberry,' he said. 'I thought that was your favourite.'

'It is.' Jordanne looked into the bowl to confirm it. 'How did you know?'

'Ah. I have my sources.' He winked at her and Jordanne's breath caught in her throat.

'Kirsten?'

Alex nodded. 'I bumped into her at the supermarket while I was trying to choose a flavour. She volunteered the information so I suspected she might know what's going on between us.'

'Is that a question?' Jordanne asked.

'Not really. I guess women love to talk.' He shrugged and didn't say anything more on the topic. They settled down to do some work, studying the information before them. Ten minutes later, the external entry door buzzer sounded. Jordanne stood up and crossed to the wall.

'Hello?

'Hi, sis. We were in the neighbourhood so we thought we'd pop in.'

Jordanne pressed the button that would release the door so Jed and Sally could come up. 'Looks as though we have company,' she said softly, her eyes trying to gauge Alex's reaction to this unexpected visit. It was one thing to let her brother know they were dating but another to actually let him see them together as a couple. Even *she* was feeling a bit nervous.

Alex didn't say anything but the easygoing atmosphere they'd previously enjoyed disappeared. His frown had returned and Jordanne could have cheerfully throttled her brother for his bad timing. Nevertheless, she opened the door when he knocked.

'Hi, sis,' her brother said as he embraced her, before walking into the room. Sally followed behind him.

'Hi.' Jordanne quickly fixed on a smile as she closed the door behind her friend. Alex stood and shook Jed's hand and kissed Sally's cheek.

'What brings you this way?' Jordanne asked.

'We've just finished a long and drawn-out operating list,' Sally answered.

'Anyone want a cup of tea?' Jed asked. Without waiting for an answer, he walked into the kitchen and put the kettle on. It was quite normal for her brother to make himself at home but Jordanne wished—just for tonight—that he and Sally would leave as soon as possible.

'Something smells good,' he said. 'Stir-fry?'

'Yes.'

'I don't suppose there's any left?' he asked as he opened the fridge to check for containers. 'I'm starving.'

'Well…' Jordanne hesitated. 'Why don't you take Sally out for dinner?'

Jed came out of the kitchen and looked from Jordanne to Alex. 'Something wrong?' His grin said that he knew he was interrupting them and he wanted to test how they reacted.

Jordanne decided the best way to approach the situation was to call his bluff. 'You can forget about it right now.'

'Forget about what?' he asked, feigning innocence. Sally laughed.

'Jed, I'm a big girl and I don't need you to check up on me.'

Jed didn't deny it. He simply grinned. 'But I wanted to see the two of you together.'

'Why?'

'Because I wanted to see how cute you are together.'

Sally laughed and Jordanne shook her head in bemusement. She glanced at Alex, whose eyebrows were raised at his friend's statement.

'Well, now you've seen us and have hopefully concluded that we're *very* cute together, so now you can leave.' Jordanne walked to the front door and held it open. She smiled sweetly at her brother. 'Goodnight, Jed. Alex and I have a lot of work to do.' She pointed to the papers on the coffee-table.

'Problem?'

'We're just going over the research project with a fine-tooth comb,' Alex supplied. 'You know, make sure all the i's are dotted and the t's crossed.'

'So my little sister's been showing off her culinary skills?' he asked, not moving from where he stood.

'Yes,' Alex answered.

Jordanne watched as Alex and Jed looked at each other. It was as though they were having a conversation solely with looks. She tried to think of something to say to break the silence but her mind had gone blank.

'All of the McElroys are good cooks,' Sally volunteered, and Jordanne could have kissed her for breaking the moment. 'And speaking of which, Jed…' She crossed to her fiancé's side and placed her hand in his. 'I'm *really* hungry. As Jordanne has no leftovers and you're probably too tired to cook, let's get take-away tonight.'

Jordanne watched as Sally tugged Jed towards the door, silently thanking her friend.

'You two get back to work before your minds start to blur from exhaustion,' Sally instructed them.

'Well, I guess we'll see you later,' Jed offered, and waved as Sally all but pushed him out the door.

As Jordanne's door closed behind them, Sally shook her head at her fiancé. 'You really shouldn't tease them like that, Jed.' They both chuckled before heading off.

Jordanne turned to look at Alex once her brother and friend had left. 'You OK?'

'Fine.' He exhaled slowly. 'I knew the first time he saw us together would seem a little…uncomfortable but, hey, it's over.' He sat down and started looking through the files again.

The kettle that Jed had switched on boiled and turned itself off. 'More coffee?' Jordanne asked, and when Alex glanced up at her he saw the worried look on her face.

'No, I'm fine.'

'Alex, say something. Tell me how you feel.' Jordanne sat down beside him, wanting desperately to touch him but not daring in case she made the situation worse.

Alex had never liked talking about his feelings to the women he'd dated in the past. He'd always put it down to not having a sister to talk to when he'd been growing up. Yet with Jordanne, the discomfort he usually felt was amazingly absent. He draped his arm around her shoulder and drew her closer.

'I just want to take things slowly,' he told her.

'OK.'

Both of them were quiet for a few more minutes before Jordanne looked at the work in front of them. 'We have to get this done.' She turned her face upwards to him, ready for a kiss. He obliged and they moved apart.

'You're right.'

Together they worked methodically, searching for something that would give them a clue as to what was going on. They studied the X-rays in detail, making notes of the dates they'd been taken.

'Call the radiography companies tomorrow and check these dates against their records,' Alex said. 'I'll get my secretary to check the referring doctors.'

Jordanne nodded and picked up the form she'd filled in for Ethan Hoe. 'So far all of the athletes have been track and field.' She looked to the line where the coach's name was written. 'Alex, who coaches Xavier Bell?'

'Ralph Cooper,' he read.

'Check the others,' Jordanne ordered. They looked at the forms for all eight athletes the company had recommended. 'They all have the same coach. Ralph Cooper.' She looked at Alex. 'Is that strange?'

'It might be.' Alex made a note of the name before looking back at the paper maze before them. 'I think that's enough for tonight. If we can check into those other areas tomorrow and discuss the findings, we'll hopefully know what's going on sooner rather than later.'

'I'm going to contact all the patients listed in the study,

apart from these athletes, and just check to see how they're going.'

'Speaking of going...' Alex stood and stretched his legs. 'We've got the private clinic in the morning and I have meetings all afternoon. Let's have dinner at my house tomorrow,' he suggested as he pulled her into his arms and placed a kiss on her lips. 'And just so you know, I like any dessert that has chocolate in it.'

Jordanne smiled up at him. 'Well, Mr Chef, I just want you to know that I don't particularly like capsicum so, please, don't cook—or order—anything with it in.'

'How does...lasagne sound?'

'Great.'

'No capsicum in that,' he teased. 'Besides, I know a great place to order from.'

'Can you cook?' she asked, a little sceptical.

'I do a mean barbeque.'

Jordanne laughed. 'You'd get on well with Justin. He loves to cook the barbeque.'

'You have so many siblings, I don't know how I'll ever remember one from the other.'

'You already know Jed and Joel. In order it goes Jed, Joel, Jasmine, Justin, me and then Jared. It's quite simple.'

He kissed her, more thoroughly this time, and Jordanne forgot about teasing him. When he finally released her, her eyes were closed and she was almost swooning. Alex chuckled as he made sure her legs would support her.

'See you tomorrow,' he whispered and kissed her again. 'I have to go,' he said a while later. Jordanne walked on wobbly legs towards the door where he kissed her one more time. 'Sleep well.'

'Mmm,' she replied, and watched dreamily as he left.

As Alex walked to his car, he reflected on the evening. The more he saw of Jordanne and the more he kissed and caressed her, the more he was willing to risk. The woman was driving him insane. Insane with desire, insane with passion, insane with needing more of anything and everything that she had to give.

He had been completely honest when he'd told her he wanted to slow their relationship down. Right now, he felt as though he was moving along like a freight train. If Jordanne McElroy *was* the woman for him, then he had a lot at stake.


'OK, Roberto,' Jordanne advised. 'You can get dressed now.' She and Alex took another look at the most recent set of Roberto's X-rays while they waited for their patient to join them.

'How does it look?' Roberto queried, and they both turned around to face him.

'Good.' Alex nodded. 'Your admission details are all organised, the equipment we require is organised.'

'Sounds as though everything is organised,' Jordanne said with a smile. 'Now, let me go over the operation with you again, so you know what you can expect before and after surgery.'

The intercom on her desk buzzed and Jordanne pressed the button.

'I have a call for Alex,' the receptionist said.

Alex looked at Roberto. 'Excuse me,' he said, before leaving the room.

Jordanne took down her plastic model of a hip and a metal prosthesis set. 'This is what we'll be doing. We need to replace this section of bone which is called the neck of femur. Your thigh bone is your femur and the hip is the upper part of the femur. So we'll be removing the bone which has been rendered almost immovable thanks to the rheumatoid arthritis. In its place, we'll be using this.' She held up the metal prosthesis set and demonstrated how they fitted together.

'It will work like new?'

'Yes, given time. Total hip replacement patients are weight-bearing one day after surgery. We need to keep your muscles good and strong to cope with the change. A physiotherapist will be assigned to you and will work with you daily. Any other questions?'

Roberto shook his head.

'Let me know if you think of some.'

'You've answered everything I wanted to know,' he told her.

'Good. Now…' She looked down at his notes. 'We have the letter from the rheumatologist, we have verification from the autologous blood clinic—'

'The what?'

Jordanne smiled. 'The place where you went to have blood taken. During the operation we need to transfuse you, and this way you can get your own blood back.'

'Oh, yes, I remember now.' Roberto nodded. 'This past week has been very busy.'

'I understand.' Jordanne smiled. She looked at his notes again. 'You've seen the anaesthetist and he's OK'd you.' She returned her gaze to Roberto. 'Is there someone who can take you to the hospital?'

'My son. He's waiting out there.'

'Good. I'll be around later this evening to check that you've settled in well. For now, that's it.'

'I'll see you then.' Roberto used his walking frame to get to the door. He'd stated that he didn't like wheelchairs and would only use one when it was absolutely necessary. 'By the way,' he said with a wide smile on his face, 'I see you've…worked things out with Dr Page. Good to see.'

Jordanne was stunned. Did their body language reveal *that* much? Roberto laughed.

'I'm an expert,' he said, as though reading her mind. 'Don't worry. I'm glad you're both so happy. Until tonight.'

That afternoon, Jordanne rang the firms who had supposedly taken X-rays of the athletes the company had referred to her. By the end of it she had a sore ear and elbow from holding the phone up for so long and a headache from listening to the awful music most of the firms had when they put people on hold.

The good news was she'd found out what she'd intended to. She grinned to herself in excitement and couldn't wait until she saw Alex that evening. It was as though they were doing a jigsaw puzzle—finding pieces here and there. She wondered how his secretary had gone with her enquiries on Alex's behalf.

Having tidied her office, Jordanne left the hospital, stopping by to see Roberto Portatello as she'd promised. He was settled quite comfortably in a private room and his family had just gone to the cafeteria to have some dinner.

She'd been there for a whole five minutes when Alex arrived.

'Why are you so bubbly with excitement?' Roberto asked her. 'Are you two going on a date tonight?'

Alex looked astonished but quickly veiled his reaction before he glared at Jordanne.

'I didn't say a word,' she said defensively, holding her hands up.

'I used to be a private investigator,' Roberto offered. 'I'm good at reading people.'

Alex nodded, only mildly satisfied with the explanation.

'So tell me,' Roberto insisted, 'I see now that it's not a date with your handsome doctor but something else.'

Jordanne looked to Alex who simply shrugged as if to say, What have we got to lose?

'Well…' Jordanne sat on the edge of his bed, her enthusiasm bubbling over. 'Alex and I are doing a research study.' Jordanne briefly outlined the basis for their research and what they'd discovered with the X-rays. 'Today I checked all of the other X-rays we've been sent and every single one has been falsified.'

'I thought so!' Alex exclaimed.

'I checked each and every date,' she told him. '*None* of them were recorded.'

'Anything else?' Roberto asked, giving them both a thoughtful look.

'All X-rays have a common association,' Jordanne told him. 'It could mean absolutely nothing.'

Roberto nodded, his eyes alive with the opportunity to help them out. It was clear to see that he had loved his previous profession. Jordanne also realised that it would help Roberto recover better from his surgery if he had something to ponder other than his present situation.

'Look for the simple connections,' he told them after a few minutes' silence. 'Don't try to make it complicated. Look for the simple clues as these are the things that will lead you to the answer.'

# CHAPTER EIGHT

JORDANNE and Alex discussed the possibilities of what might be going on with the study for quite some time as they ate dinner that night. Finally, Alex stood and went into the kitchen to start clearing up.

'It's good to see a man barefoot in the kitchen with his hands in soapy water,' Jordanne teased. The phone rang.

'Don't worry. I'll get it.' Before he could say another word, Jordanne had picked up the receiver. 'Dr Page's residence,' she said in a shrill English accent. There was silence on the end of the line. 'Hello?' she said in her normal voice.

A deep chuckle rumbled down the line. 'That has got to be Jordanne McElroy,' the voice said.

Jordanne frowned. 'And this is?'

'Scott—Alex's brother.'

'Scott,' Jordanne said slowly, nodding and looking at Alex. 'So how come you know about me, Scott?'

Alex had taken his hands out of the sink and dried them quickly before snatching the receiver from Jordanne.

'Hey, bro,' he said. 'Can I call you back?'

Scott chuckled down the line. 'Caught you at a bad time, did I? Way to go, big brother.'

'Goodbye, Scott,' Alex said between clenched teeth before hanging up.

'So?' Jordanne looked at him in surprise. 'Have you been telling your brother all about me?' She advanced slowly towards Alex.

'I haven't told Scott anything.'

'Oh,' she said, not believing a word he said. 'I suppose he's very good at reading people, just like Roberto Portatello is.'

'Something like that,' Alex said, now hard up against the kitchen cupboard. Jordanne was enjoying herself.

'I didn't think my memory was *that* bad. I could have sworn I'd never met your brother.'

'You haven't,' he said as Jordanne pressed her body against his. He loved it when she was in this type of playful mood.

She kissed his neck. 'I suppose Scott has…' she added a few more kisses, teasing him lightly with her lips '…read your mind and…' a few more kisses '…found out my name.'

'Ah.' Alex hesitated as her kisses started moving upwards to his face. 'Something like that,' he repeated in a whisper as her mouth finally reached his. His lips caught hers as his arms came around, holding her firmly in an embrace.

Jordanne felt a burning need rip through her being as she gave everything to the kiss. How she loved to be with Alex, to tease him and joke with him. How she loved working alongside him, in clinics, meetings and Theatre. How she loved him—full stop.

Jordanne eased back and looked at him. The desire and need were evident in his gaze and she *loved* seeing it there. She watched as it slowly cooled before disappearing. He was withdrawing again and it wasn't the first time he'd done it.

He kissed the tip of her nose and set her from him before returning to the sink.

Slowly does it, she told herself as she picked up the drying towel to help him with the dishes. 'Have you ever thought about investing in a dishwasher?' she asked, and to her surprise he looked at her and smiled. Jordanne felt her knees go weak with the desire that was still simmering below the surface. 'What?' she asked when he didn't say anything.

'I quite like doing the dishes,' he responded, and the awkward moment passed. 'I guess it gives me a sense of control in an otherwise chaotic society.'

'You get all of that from doing dishes?' Jordanne asked with a laugh. 'Maybe you've been inhaling too many of those soap suds.' When his rich laughter filled the room, she was glad that she'd been able to make him smile again.

They ate dinner at Jordanne's place the following evening after a busy public clinic in the morning and operating on Roberto Portatello in the afternoon, the surgery going off without complications.

On Friday morning in the private practice there was a knock on Jordanne's consulting-room door, not long after her final patient had left. Alex came in without waiting for her to answer.

'I just received this,' he said, and held out an envelope to her.

'Oh, is the mail in? Is there a letter about—'

'Yes, the mail's in but forget about that. Do you know anything about this?'

Jordanne took the proffered envelope from him and recognised the handwriting on the front as her mother's. 'It's an invitation to my parents' wedding anniversary party next Saturday.' Jordanne was just as surprised as Alex. She matched his frown. 'I didn't know anything about it. You getting an invitation, I mean. Of course I knew about the party. Mum's been planning it for ages.'

'So you didn't tell your parents to invite me?'

'No. I *had* planned to bring you *with* me.'

'Then why did I get an invitation?'

'Well, they know we're dating and my mother probably didn't want you to feel left out but I certainly didn't *tell* her to invite you. Mum probably figured you'd want your own invitation, especially as you missed Jed's big birthday bash a month or so ago.'

'But I've never met your parents.'

'Haven't you? That's weird. You and Jed have been friends for such a long time, yet you've never met our parents.'

'I have lots of friends and colleagues and I don't know any of *their* parents either.'

Jordanne indicated the chair behind him. 'Why don't you sit down and we can discuss this further?'

'I don't want to sit down.' He started pacing around her office. 'So your parents know that we're dating.'

'Yes.'

'I thought we were taking it slow.'

'Telling my parents increases the rate of our relationship?' Jordanne asked in amazement.

Alex raked a hand through his hair. 'Look Jordanne. Things are progressing way too quickly and there are some things we need to talk about.'

Jordanne felt a hand tighten around her heart, constricting it from movement at his words. 'OK,' she said carefully. 'Why don't you sit down?'

'No.' He shook his head for emphasis. 'We can't talk here. How about we go out for dinner tonight?'

'Out?' This was more serious than she'd thought. Tears started to well behind her eyes and she instantly willed them away. Every other night this week they'd eaten either at his house or hers but tonight, when he wanted to *talk* to her, he wanted to go out. Her intuition told her it wasn't a good idea and the suspicion that he was going to break up with her grew stronger. He obviously thought that if they were in a public place when he broke the news she wouldn't make a scene.

Jordanne swallowed the lump in her throat. 'Uh…but we're on call.' Her voice sounded flat even to her own ears.

'We'll have our mobile phones with us.'

'All right. Why don't you pick me up just after seven?'

'Sounds good. I have a sub-committee meeting which usually runs late.' He glanced at the clock on her wall. 'Are you heading off to the IAS soon?'

'Yes.' Jordanne cleared her throat and looked down at her desk. 'I just have to finish typing up my notes on the last patient and dictate a letter before I'm ready to go.'

'I'm on my way to the hospital for a meeting now, so I'll see you tonight.'

He walked around her desk and bent to kiss her briefly before turning and heading towards the door. He stopped and looked at her again. 'Are you planning on speaking to Coach Cooper this afternoon?'

'Yes.'

'Would you mind waiting?'

'Why? So you can come with me? I can handle the man by myself, Alex.' Her words came out harshly and she knew she was just trying to cover up her vulnerability.

'It's not that.'

'He's the common factor with the eight athletes the company have recommended and I think he knows what's going on here. The sooner I talk to him, the sooner I'm going to get some answers.'

'What makes you think you're going to get answers?' Alex responded.

Jordanne thought about it for a moment. 'You think I should wait?' she asked, seeing his point.

'Yes. I can't say why, it's just a gut reaction.'

She nodded, respecting his opinion. 'OK. I'll cancel my appointment.'

'Thanks. See you tonight.'

Jordanne pushed all thoughts about what Alex wanted to discuss that night to the back of her mind and forced herself to concentrate on the research project. It was true that the more they uncovered, the more intriguing it became. On the other hand, they didn't know what they might be getting themselves into.

She reread the patient information she'd taken from all of the participants in the study, not just the athletes from the company, desperately trying to find some hidden clue. After a few hours her vision was blurring and her head was aching, although she presumed that was from trying to keep her thoughts off Alex. Deciding she needed to stretch her legs, she locked her office and headed over to the library.

'Hi, there,' Sky said as Jordanne walked in the door. 'I was just going to phone you. I have a parcel for you.'

'Really? Hope it's something nice.'

'I think it's that new book you ordered.'

'Excellent.'

'Oh, and these came for you also,' Sky said, handing over two envelopes of blood test results.

'Thanks.' Jordanne put them to one side and opened up the parcel. 'About time, too,' she said as she pulled the book out. She glanced through a few of the pages before closing it again. 'Sky? Those X-rays you sent to me the other day, did they arrive via courier?'

'Yes.'

'Can you remember which one?'

'It's all documented here,' Sky said as she pulled out a file. 'This has a record of all incoming deliveries and any parcels I send out.'

Jordanne read the log. 'VF Couriers. What does the VF stand for?' she asked.

'Very Fast?' Sky shrugged. 'I don't know. The only time I've had them deliver here is when I have stuff coming in from the pharmaceutical company who pays your research grant.'

Jordanne made a note of the details. 'Thanks.'

'Something wrong?'

'Everything's fine.'

'Hey, here's our gold medallist,' Sky said as Sally walked into the library. Jordanne knew that Sky liked to tease Sally about the gold medal she'd won in the Olympics when she'd been a teenager, and as it was all in fun Sally didn't mind.

The three of them stood around chatting for a few minutes, Jordanne and Sally grilling Sky about the new man in her life. It was a welcome change to concentrate on someone else's romance, Jordanne thought as she listened to Sky rave about the new biomedical engineer who had stolen her heart.

'He's from Sri Lanka,' Sky enthused. 'I just love his dark brown eyes. I could drown in them.' She sighed.

'Blue eyes for me,' Sally and Jordanne said in unison, and they all laughed.

'This isn't going to get the work done,' Jordanne complained as she gathered up the book and the blood-test results.

'I just came by to check my pigeonhole,' Sally said, and did exactly that.

'Good idea.' Jordanne followed suit. 'Have a good weekend, Sky,' she called as Sally held the door for her. The two friends walked back towards their research offices.

'How's the study going?' Sally asked.

'It's…interesting. There are a few discrepancies that I

want to clear up but otherwise *very* interesting. Hey, aren't you and Jed off to Sydney tonight?'

'Yes. It's all very exciting and I'm looking forward to it.' They stopped outside Sally's office door which was just down the corridor from Jordanne's. 'Sorry about the other night and us barging in on you two like that.'

'That's OK.' Jordanne hugged her friend a bit tighter than usual.

'Something wrong?' Sally asked.

'Nothing I can't handle. You and Jed have a great time this weekend.' Jordanne forced a smile.

'We will.'

'Say hi to Mum and Dad for me, as well as your parents.'

'I will, but right now I'd better get the rest of my work done or I won't be going anywhere.'

'Agreed,' Jordanne said, and once Sally had gone, she sat down in her chair and opened the first of the test results. 'Ethan Hoe's. Good,' she mumbled to herself. She scanned the printout, pleased to see that everything checked out. Opening the second envelope, she frowned. '*More* test results for Ethan Hoe?' Jordanne shook her head. What was going on?

'Dr McElroy?' a voice said from her open doorway, and Jordanne literally sprang out of her chair in fright. She pressed her hand to her chest as she tried to calm her breathing down, her gaze taking in the man before her.

He had bleached blond hair, grey eyes and the body of a very well-trained athlete, even though she guessed him to be well into his fifties.

'I'm Ralph Cooper.' He didn't hold out his hand or apologise for scaring the life out of her. Jordanne looked at him for another moment before lowering her hand from her chest.

'We had an appointment?'

'Oh, my gosh, I meant to call you and cancel. Sorry,' she said, still wary of him. He didn't venture into her office. 'I've been absorbed in my work,' she babbled, indicating her desk. His gaze dropped to look where she pointed before returning to her.

'I hope there's nothing wrong with my athletes,' he stated rather than asked.

'No. At this stage, everything seems fine.'

'Good, because it cuts into their training regime if they have to come here *every month* and have you stick needles into them.'

'It's only one needle and it's for a simple blood test,' Jordanne said defensively.

'I need to get back to the track.' Without another word, he left. Jordanne stood where she was for a full two minutes, open-mouthed and amazed at the man's appalling attitude.

'He was so completely and utterly *rude*,' Jordanne told Alex as they ate dinner that night. 'He looked at me as though I wasn't worth a thing.'

'Some coaches are like that,' Alex said. 'If you're not an athlete, if you don't live, eat and breathe sport, then you're not worth knowing. I'm not defending him or making excuses for his rudeness,' he added quickly as Jordanne opened her mouth to protest.

'I wish I'd cancelled my meeting with him,' she grumbled. 'I was just so preoccupied with those false X-rays that I forgot. I'm so cross with myself.'

Alex reached across the table and took Jordanne's hand in his. He gave it a little squeeze. 'Don't be. From what you've said of his attitude, he might well be trying to hide something. Remember what Roberto said, don't make things too complicated. Also, steer clear of Ralph Cooper from now on.'

'My pleasure,' Jordanne said, and forced herself to smile. 'I'm going to forget that project for a few hours and just enjoy being with you.' Taking a sip of her wine, she said, 'Although I would like to go over the test results I received today.'

'Is that the envelope you've left in my glovebox?'

'Yes. Hopefully, we'll be able to come up with some-thing—*anything*—to help bring us closer to understanding what's going on.'

Alex smiled at her.

'What?' she asked with a slight frown.

'I thought you weren't going to think about the research project for a while.'

'Sorry.'

He shook his head. 'No apologies necessary. Now, what shall we order for dessert?'

Jordanne had been expecting him to drop a bombshell as soon as he'd picked her up, but his mood had been quite jovial, if a little reserved, since they'd entered the restaurant. She wondered whether he was trying to lull her into a false sense of security but couldn't figure out any reason why he'd want to do that. Right now she was just puzzled by his earlier declaration that he wanted to talk.

'How about…?' Jordanne studied the menu the waiter had just brought over. 'Ooh, chocolate fondue. It's been years since I had fondue—and you like chocolate.'

'That I do. Sounds perfect.' Alex motioned to the waiter who quickly returned to their table. He gave the order and when the waiter had gone Alex raised his glass in a toast.

'Here's to chocolate-covered fruit—able to make anyone forget their troubles for a while.'

'Hear! hear!' Jordanne felt the anvil of doom begin to fall at his words but she went through the motion of chink-ing her glass with his, acknowledging the toast.

She forced herself to enjoy the fondue, playing by the rules she had learned in college—that if you dropped a piece of fruit into the fondue, you had to kiss the closest person to you.

'You seem to be dropping an awful lot of fruit,' she told Alex after he'd kissed her once more. How could he possibly break it off with her? The way he was acting tonight, it was as though he was happy about their relationship.

'Any excuse will do,' he said, before eating a chocolate-covered strawberry.

'Who says you need an excuse?' she quipped.

'You're right.' And with that, Alex promptly kissed her again. Jordanne licked the chocolate from her lips, feeling very happy. When they'd finished, Alex paid the bill and they walked outside into the cool September breeze.

'Thank you for dinner,' Jordanne said, linking her fingers with his. It was getting late now and the streets weren't quite as busy as they'd been when they'd first entered the restaurant. Still, there were a few cars parked along the side of the road. Alex, however, had chosen a patrolled car-parking station to leave the Jaguar which was a few short blocks away.

Alex looked down at her briefly before unlinking his fingers and placing his arm about her shoulders. She'd chosen a sensible trouser suit to wear this evening, instead of another sexy dress.

'Jordanne, as I said earlier today, we need to talk.'

Jordanne swallowed the lump that had immediately formed itself in her throat. 'OK.'

'I'm quite a bit older than you,' he said, his tone very serious.

'Eight years. Same as Sally and Jed.'

'Yes, but eight years can make all the difference earlier on in life.'

Jordanne frowned and looked up at him as they continued to walk along.

He took a deep breath in before saying, 'I'm divorced.'

'What?' She stopped, unable to believe what he'd just said. 'Divorced?' she repeated, making sure she'd heard correctly.

He nodded. 'It was a long time—'

A squeal of tyres interrupted him and they both turned around to look. An old, battered, orange car was fishtailing down the road and Alex edged Jordanne back towards the building side of the footpath.

'He'd better slow down,' Alex murmured. 'Before he has an acc—'

No sooner had he said the words than the car swerved out of control and smashed into another car parked on the road. Ricocheting off, the orange car spun a few times before veering to the other side of the road where it smashed into another car. The orange car was now facing the direction it had come from.

Police sirens could be heard and within seconds a patrol car, red and blue lights flashing, rounded the corner with a squeal. Alex urged Jordanne back even further, into a small entryway to one of the buildings.

Jordanne looked at him with surprise as he shielded her body with his. She smiled to herself. It was such an instinctively protective reaction that she couldn't help but be touched by the sweet gesture. She was becoming more accustomed to the effect his close proximity had on her equilibrium but also knew she'd *never* grow tired of it.

Together they peered around the corner, watching the police car brake suddenly and swerve. Both officers started to get out but Jordanne noticed that the driver of the orange car had opened his door and was crouching behind it. A shot rang out into the evening, causing one officer to dive back into the car and the other to crouch down behind it.

Jordanne gasped with shock, her eyes wide in stunned amazement. She was now very glad that she and Alex were hidden in the dark shadows, out of sight.

The second officer crawled through the car and out the other side and soon they opened fire. Jordanne's heart hammered wildly against her ribs. She wasn't sure whether it was from the excitement around them or the closeness of Alex's firm, muscled body against her own. She breathed in sharply and her senses were pleasantly assaulted with the wonderful scent of Alex's cologne.

The red and blue lights were still whizzing around, scattering their colours on the surrounding buildings. From where Jordanne and Alex were sheltered, they could see more of what the police were doing than the gunman.

'Hold your fire,' one of the officers called.

'Yeah, right,' Jordanne said out the corner of her mouth. The gunman's answer was a shot that hit the front windscreen of the car.

More shots from the police as they returned fire. Another siren could be heard wailing in the distance, getting closer with each passing second.

Jordanne watched as the police fired again and this time they heard a muffled noise from the gunman that echoed around the now empty street as the bullets struck home. The sound of the man's weapon clattered to the ground as he slumped down, his body motionless.

'I feel sick,' she said, her head pounding in agony at the thought of a man being shot.

'Don't pass out on me,' Alex ordered.

'I won't,' Jordanne told him. 'I never faint.'

'Good. Hopefully, they've already called for an ambulance.' They both turned in the direction of the siren as another police car came down the street. The first two officers were making their way slowly towards the gunman, their guns trained on him in case he was faking.

Jordanne and Alex stood up, crossing towards the second car. The policemen got out, their guns pointed at Jordanne and Alex.

Alex put his hands in the air, Jordanne followed suit.

'We're doctors,' he called as they slowly advanced towards the police car. By now they were close enough for the police to see them.

'Got some ID?' the cop called.

'Inside suit pocket,' Alex replied, but didn't attempt to get it out. He let the policeman come over, his partner's gun still trained on them both. He waited until the policeman was satisfied.

'Fine, you can lower your hands,' he ordered. 'What about you?' He motioned to Jordanne.

'It's in here,' she said, indicating the small bag that was looped around her shoulder, hanging diagonally across her body.

When the policeman had cleared her as well, he said, 'The ambulance should be here soon. Let's go check out the situation.'

Jordanne and Alex followed but were told to wait until the all-clear had been given. Finally, they were able to attend to the gunman. 'Gunshot wound to right femur and right humerus,' she said to the cops as Alex checked the man's vital signs.

'Is he stable?'

'No. Femur wounds are bad. He's already lost a lot of blood. First-aid kit?' she enquired, knowing one would be in the police car. They bandaged him up as best they could but the man needed a blood transfusion and an IV line in— quickly. His fluids would be getting dangerously low.

'Is that the ambulance?' Alex asked as another siren pierced the hum that now surrounded the street. The police had cordoned off the area as people came out of shops and restaurants to have a look.

The paramedics gave the gunman an anaesthetic and rigged up an IV line. Alex rode in the back of the ambulance with a police officer while Jordanne sat between the paramedics.

Finally, when they reached the hospital, she and Alex headed for Theatres to organise equipment and get changed. Jordanne looked down at one of her favourite suits which now had bloodstains over it. 'Oh, well, part and parcel of the job,' she mumbled to herself.

Mr Oswald Miner, as they'd been informed, was the gunman's name and he wasn't in good shape. Together Alex and Jordanne removed the bullet from the femur and tied off a severed artery that was causing the blood loss. After receiving two units of blood and some Haemaccel, Mr Miner was stabilised.

Finally, they were ready for the check X-rays. When Alex was satisfied with the views he said, 'Let's proceed.' They debrided the wound, before plating the bone back together. The humerus was attended to in a similar fashion and after eight hours in Theatre Jordanne and Alex walked wearily out. 'Coffee?'

'I don't think I have the energy to lift the cup,' Jordanne replied as she slumped down into one of the chairs in the ESS doctors' tearoom. There was a knock on the open door and one of the policemen from the scene walked into the room.

'How'd it go?'

'He's in Recovery. He'll go to Intensive Care tonight and then to the ward in a few days' time.'

'He's a known felon. There are four warrants out for his

arrest. I'll need to organise a guard to be near him all the time.'

'Fair enough.' Alex nodded. 'I guess we can't do the paperwork in the morning?'

'Sorry. I need the guard around him tonight.'

'Even if he *wanted* to escape, the man can't even move, let alone walk.'

'Still…'

'No, I understand.' He glanced across at Jordanne who shrugged. 'Let's get on with it, then.'

Another hour later, Jordanne changed into clean theatre scrubs as her suit was now unwearable. Alex was waiting for her near the door to the emergency surgical suite. 'Ready?' he said.

'Mmm.' She nodded.

'We'll have to take a taxi to the parking station to collect my car,' he said, and Jordanne simply nodded again. She was too tired to argue and too tired to care. Alex held her hand in the taxi and when they were in his car she dozed as he drove towards her apartment.

'Jordanne? Come on, honey. Wake up,' he crooned when they'd arrived.

'Hmm?' she said, opening half-sleepy eyes to gaze at him. 'I like it when you call me honey,' she slurred sleepily.

He smiled. 'Let's get you inside. Where are your keys?'

Jordanne managed to get them out and handed them to Alex. He held her close as they walked up the one flight of stairs to her door. He unlocked the door with his free hand and ushered her in.

Flicking on the light switch, they both blinked in rapid succession. Not because their eyes weren't used to the bright overhead lights but because Jordanne's place was in a mess and it was definitely *not* the way she'd left it earlier that evening.

'I've been robbed!' she breathed in shock.

# CHAPTER NINE

JORDANNE looked around the room in shock. Tears of fury blurred her eyes and she brushed them away impatiently. 'How?' She spread her arms wide and shook her head. 'Why?' That was the next question out of her mouth.

Alex turned around and checked the door again. 'There's no sign of forced entry. Maybe they didn't come in through the door.'

'How did they get into the building?' Jordanne asked, her tone rising slightly. She could feel hysteria bubbling within her and if she wasn't careful it would boil over.

'I'll check your windows.' Alex stepped over the side-table and lamp which had been knocked down before heading to the other rooms. Jordanne walked forward in a daze, taking in the mess around the room. Her entire bookshelf had been emptied of its contents and it looked as though each book had been shaken open before being dumped unceremoniously onto the ground.

She sighed heavily and started to pick up some books and put them back on the shelf before Alex walked back into the room.

'Don't touch them,' he said, and she dropped them like hot potatoes back to the floor.

'What's wrong?'

'We have to call the police. Just leave the room the way it is until they get here.'

Alex lifted the receiver from her phone. 'It's dead,' he said in surprise. He took his mobile from his waistband and made the call.

'None of this makes any sense,' Jordanne whispered to herself.

'It's all right,' he said after disconnecting and crossing to her side. The instant Alex enveloped her in his arms, Jordanne finally gave way to the tears that had been threatening since she'd first caught a glimpse of her apartment.

'Shh.'

It felt good to have Alex there, stroking her hair and holding her close. Jordanne was amazed at how quickly she had come to rely on him in such a short time. She guessed it was due to the fact that she loved him—one hundred per cent. Her arms tightened around him as her tears slowly subsided.

'Thank you,' she whispered through her hiccups.

'You don't have to thank me for anything, Jordanne,' Alex said before he claimed her lips. Jordanne clung to him, gaining strength from the arms that held her and the kisses that relaxed her nerves.

'You're so good for me,' she told him when they finally parted. Right at this moment, she didn't care about his past. It was just that—past. She took a deep breath and slowly exhaled. 'How long do you think it will be until the police arrive?'

'No idea.'

'Do you think they'd mind if we disturbed the coffee-cups and kettle in the kitchen?'

Alex smiled. 'Probably not.' He released her but still held onto her fingers as they walked into the kitchen. 'Just from looking around the room, can you see anything that might be missing?' he asked as they waited for the jug to boil. The kitchen wasn't as messy as the lounge room.

'The TV's there, so is the VCR and the stereo.' She ticked them off on her fingers. 'What does my bedroom look like?'

'There are clothes everywhere. You can hardly see your bed.'

Jordanne sighed thankfully and smiled at him. 'Whew! At least *that's* the way I left it.'

Alex's laughter rumbled from deep in his chest. 'You're one amazing woman, Jordanne McElroy,' he told her as he watched her make them coffee. 'To make light of the situation at a time like this.'

Jordanne was glad for something to do as she put three sugars into her coffee. She needed it tonight—or rather this morning. 'Who's kidding? That's the way I usually get dressed. I can never make up my mind what to wear, especially when I'm seeing you.'

'How long did it take you to choose that red dress you wore last week?'

'Ah, now, that was different. My bedroom looked quite tidy *that* night.'

'Well, from what I could see, your jewellery boxes are all still there, although I didn't check the contents.'

'Should I do that before the police arrive?' She sipped at her sickly sweet coffee. 'You know, get together a list of what's missing?'

'Might be an idea,' he said. 'Just try not to move things too much.'

There was a buzz from the external intercom. 'Could be them now,' Jordanne said, her previous nervousness returning.

Alex answered the intercom and let the police in. They took a brief look around the room before asking questions, especially about why Jordanne was dressed in theatre garb. An hour and a half later Jordanne and Alex said goodbye to the police, who had filled in so many forms they'd decided it was worse than hospital red tape.

'I don't think I can face this right now.' Jordanne shook her head, still gazing in wonderment at the mess before her.

'Pack some things and come back to my place for the night,' Alex suggested. When she looked at him quizzically he held up his hands in defence. 'I'm exhausted—you're exhausted. We'll just *sleep*,' he emphasised.

Jordanne smiled gratefully at him. 'Thank you.' She ventured back into her room, still amazed that she hadn't found anything missing. The police had been certain that whoever had broken in had been looking for something very specific. 'But what?' she whispered to herself as she packed a small bag of clothes and toiletries. Jordanne reached for her long coat as it was quite cool outside and put it on. It would also disguise the theatre clothes she was still wearing.

'Ready,' she said as she re-entered the room. She stood by the front door and glanced sadly around the mess once more before she and Alex left.

It was dawn when they arrived at his place. Jordanne was feeling a little nervous at accepting his suggestion. 'You go first in the bathroom and get into bed,' he instructed. 'I'm going to make you a soothing milk drink to help you sleep.' With that he disappeared into the kitchen.

She'd half expected him to show her to a guest bed and had been surprised when he'd indicated his own bed. 'It's the only one in the house,' he'd told her. 'You're the only overnight visitor I've ever had.'

That in itself told Jordanne a lot about his previous relationships. She tied up her hair, deciding that at this time of the morning it would not be a good idea to wash it. It took ages to dry. After taking off her clothes, she stepped under the shower and began to soap her body. Slowly her tired muscles started to relax beneath the hot spray of the water.

Jordanne thought about Alex and the way he kept a part

of himself distant from everyone and everything. She couldn't put her finger on exactly what was wrong but she sensed it was there. She'd been very surprised when he'd told her he'd been divorced. Jed had never said anything but, then, it was hardly a topic to bring up in casual conversation.

The knowledge that he'd also never had an overnight guest before made her feel...special. Turning off the water, she dried herself before dressing for bed. After brushing her teeth and hair, she climbed between the sheets of the king-size bed and snuggled down. She could smell Alex's scent on the pillows and her insides fluttered at the thought of him sleeping beside her.

When he returned, he placed the drink on the bedside table and looked down at her. 'Jordanne,' he whispered, and reached out a hand to touch her hair which was fanned over the pillow.

Her eyes closed at his touch and she sighed. She heard him straighten and clear his throat. 'Don't fall asleep *just* yet,' he said when she didn't open her eyes. 'I want that drink all gone by the time I've finished in the bathroom,' he told her as he disappeared behind the door.

Jordanne forced her weighted eyelids to open before wriggling up to take a sip. It was delicious and she could easily taste the brandy he'd added. Obeying his orders, she finished the drink, snuggled back down beneath the covers and closed her eyes. Sleep claimed her instantly.

The ringing of a telephone penetrated Jordanne's hazy mind and she struggled to wake. There was something around her, holding her tight. Was it the sheets? Moving her fingers, she came into contact with hard muscled torso and her eyes snapped open in alarm. Then her memory returned with a thud.

Her apartment had been wrecked and she was at Alex's house. In Alex's bed. With Alex's arms securely around her. The ringing of the phone persisted and she tapped him quickly.

'Alex. Phone,' she whispered as she moved from his grasp.

'Hmm?' He breathed in deeply. 'Jordanne.' Her name was like a caress on his lips and she smiled.

'Wake up, sleepyhead. Your phone is ringing.' No sooner were the words out of her mouth than it stopped.

'See. Leave it long enough and the answering machine can do its job.'

'You'd better check it,' Jordanne said as she plumped the pillows up and leaned back against the bedhead. In the next instant, there was a chorus of ringing phones. 'That's my mobile,' she said as she flipped back the sheets and padded over to the chair where her bag was.

'Mine, too,' he said, and followed Jordanne's example. 'Something must be wrong,' he stated as they both answered their mobiles. Jordanne walked into the hallway so she could hear properly. After ending the call, she returned to his room.

'No rest for us this morning,' he told her as his gaze quickly scanned the generous amount of leg revealed beneath her thigh-length T-shirt. 'How long will it take you to get ready?

'A few minutes. What's the time?' she asked, glancing at his bedside clock. 'Ten a.m.!'

'Relax, Jordanne. It's Saturday. I didn't think it was necessary to set the alarm as neither of us had any clinics or meetings to go to.'

'Instead, we now have to return to Theatre with Mr Miner,' Jordanne said as she gathered up her clothes and headed towards the bathroom.

Seven minutes later, both of them were in Alex's Jaguar, heading for the hospital. 'Volkmann's ischaemic contracture. I haven't seen one of them for a while.'

'Compartment syndrome of the upper arm,' he clarified.

'All the symptoms the ICU staff reported point to it. Progressive pain, not being relieved by analgesics...'

'Can't extend fingers properly,' Alex added.

'Mild numbness and tingling,' Jordanne finished. 'Did you request they do a urine test?'

'Yes. I also said I wanted a rush on the results. We need to relieve the pressure immediately. You go to ESS and organise the theatre and I'll head to ICU.'

'OK. I'll stay down in ESS so page me when you're ready.'

Alex pulled into the emergency parking bay and tossed his keys to an orderly who would park it in the doctors' car park for him. Both he and Jordanne went about their respective duties and soon Oswald Miner was back in Theatre, the police still standing guard outside.

'Good morning, ladies and gentlemen,' Alex said to the staff. 'Mr Miner has a complication from his earlier surgery and it's our duty to remedy it. An incision to relieve the excessive pressure from his muscles will be needed to restore the circulation.'

'You're in a good mood this morning, Alex,' theatre sister said as the last drape was put in place.

'Is that a complaint, Sister?' Alex asked.

'Not at all.'

'Glad to hear it. I'm ready to make the incision,' he said, and soon they were well into the operation. Jordanne smiled beneath her mask as she concentrated on her work.

Less than an hour later Mr Miner was wheeled out of Theatre and into Recovery, the ever-present policeman guarding him.

'What'll happen next?' the officer in charge of the case asked Alex and Jordanne.

'The incision in his arm will remain open for the next few days to allow the area to heal properly. Then we'll take him back to Theatre and close the wound,' Alex explained.

'So he'll make a full recovery.'

'I don't see why not.'

'Good.'

'Let's have another brainstorming session about this research project,' Alex suggested when he and Jordanne had been left alone.

'Good idea,' she replied as she headed for the female changing rooms.

'I'll meet you in my office. Do you want me to get those test results from my car?'

'Yes. Thanks.' They stopped in exactly the same place they'd been when Alex had first kissed her. He looked down the corridor and saw a theatre nurse heading in their direction. His gaze returned to Jordanne's and he simply nodded and went into the males' changing rooms.

Jordanne sighed as she changed back into her clothes. She'd seen the few raised eyebrows when they'd arrived together but hoped that the brother-and-sister rumour she'd started would protect them. Ironic, she thought as she brushed out her hair before quickly braiding it. She'd started that rumour to get closer to Alex but now it was serving as a cover for what was *really* going on between them.

He was in his office, just about to open the test results, when she walked in. At least the department was deserted on the weekend so they were assured of peace and quiet. Jordanne brought a chair around and sat beside him.

She pointed to the first set of results 'Look at these,' she said. 'These were the first lot I looked at. Everything appears normal.'

'Uh-huh.'

'Then I opened the next envelope and again they're blood test results for Ethan Hoe. Dates and times are the same but look at these results.'

'His red blood cell count has *dramatically* increased,' Alex commented.

'Why do you think we have two lots of test results showing a massive discrepancy? What's your gut reaction?' Jordanne asked.

'Doping,' he stated quietly, and she nodded in agreement.

'That's what I thought. Someone is trying to cover up doping.' A picture of Coach Cooper formed in her mind and she scowled. 'Ordinarily, I'd say that it might have been a misprint, but to receive two lots of test results, both taken from the same blood sample—'

'We can't be sure of that,' Alex interjected. 'Look at the X-rays.'

'Good point but, again, why were the X-rays falsified if someone wasn't trying to cover something up? With professional athletes, doping seems the obvious answer.'

'They'd be asked to leave the IAS and their careers as professional athletes would be over.'

'Why are *we* getting all this information? From the few things that Coach Cooper said to me, it was obvious that he didn't appreciate his athletes spending time taking part in this study.'

'It must have something to do with our study.'

'But what?'

'Let's start from the beginning.' Alex stood and paced around his office. 'The research project is to monitor the healing process of long bones. When I was applying for funding, the pharmaceutical company almost jumped on the bandwagon. I thought it was good that they were eager— now I'm not so sure. I also required funding to pay your wage,' he pointed out. '*If* there's anything illegal going on here, we both need to realise that by blowing the lid off it you'll lose your job.'

A lump of lead thumped into Jordanne's heart at his words. She'd have to leave Canberra unless she could get a job somewhere else, but contracts weren't due to be offered for at least another three to four months.

'Putting that thought aside, we have falsified X-rays and now falsified test results—but *only* from the athletes that the pharmaceutical company have recommended.'

'Perhaps the tablets we're giving them are being doctored in some way? Taking part in the study might be just the cover-up they need.'

Alex nodded. 'The X-rays were our first clue. How was the company to know that Dylan Foster was a patient of ours? They didn't. Someone at the radiography company must be working for them, but it was a pretty stupid error to make as your name would have been on Dylan's films as the referring doctor.' He crossed to his desk and picked up the test results. 'And now these.' Alex exhaled slowly as he sat down again and linked his fingers behind his head. 'All of this is pure speculation. We need evidence. I'll check the internet to see who's listed as the parent company for the pharmaceutical company. That might help. You could take a look at Ethan Hoe's medical history, which should be in the IAS database.'

Jordanne stood. 'I might have brought the notes I made on him back to my office here, I can't remember. Let me check.' Jordanne retrieved her keys and headed down the corridor to her office. Unlocking the door, she crossed to her desk and riffled through a few piles of papers. 'Maybe in the filing cabinet,' she murmured to herself. She went to unlock it but found it already open. 'Odd.' When she pulled the drawer open she gasped, before yelling, 'Alex!' Her tone carried disbelief and anger.

'What is it?' he called as he came quickly down the corridor.

'My files are in different places and the cabinet was unlocked.' Jordanne glanced around the room as Alex came over to check it out. 'The Monet's moved.' She pointed to the wall where the Monet had previously hung opposite her desk so she could relax when sitting down. 'The paintings have been switched. The Monet is supposed to hang there, not the painting my sister did.'

'Right. Don't touch anything. I'll call the police—*again*.'

They managed to get hold of Senior Sergeant Dorne, who had conducted the investigation at Jordanne's house. He came down to the hospital and checked out her office.

'Do you own a car?'

'Yes.' Jordanne hadn't even *thought* about her car. The last time she'd driven it had been home on Friday after she'd finished work. Since then she'd been chauffeured around by Alex.

'Any other places of residence? Offices?'

'I have an office at the IAS,' Jordanne offered.

'We'll need to have a look at that, too. As I said before, it looks as though someone is looking for something specific and it's something they're almost positive *you* have.' He pointed to Jordanne as he said it.

'Why don't you take the sergeant to the IAS and check things out there?' Alex suggested. 'Then come back here and we can have a debrief—try and see if we can't sort this thing out.'

'You have some ideas of who might be doing this?' Dorne asked Alex.

He nodded. 'We'll talk about it when you return,' he said.

Jordanne's office at the IAS looked almost as bad as her apartment. At least her office at the hospital hadn't been annihilated. 'Can you think of anything these people might have been looking for?' Dorne asked.

'Let me just check something out on the computer,' she said, avoiding his question. He watched her closely as she navigated through the files, bringing up Ethan Hoe's record. She printed the information out and picked up the X-rays—both those of Dylan Foster and, supposedly, Ethan Hoe.

As they returned to the hospital, Dorne received a call about Jordanne's car. It *had* been broken into but nothing appeared to be missing.

'Just as I'd suspected,' he told her.

When they were all seated in Alex's office, his gaze met Jordanne's. She read regret and anguish in his eyes and wondered what was going on. Alex explained their earlier suspicions to the senior sergeant, who took notes and looked at the evidence of falsified blood tests and X-rays. They definitely had his attention now.

'How did Ethan's previous medical history check out?' Dorne asked, and Jordanne handed him the printout. They carefully scanned it together.

Alex nodded as though he was reading exactly what he'd expected to see. 'A perfect blood test every time. Look at his red blood cell count after the last doping test—perfect.'

'You mean he's already been tested for doping?' Dorne asked.

'All of the athletes,' Jordanne explained, 'undergo a test every four months. The Institute of Australasian Sport prides themselves on a zero dope policy. Unfortunately, a lot of athletes and coaches know how to get around the system.'

'So what does his red blood cell count have to do with it?'

'If an athlete is taking a performance-enhancing drug, their red blood cell count is dramatically elevated. In Ethan Hoe's case, as we have two sets of differing test results, we'd like him to provide a urine sample so we can clarify it.'

'But if he's taking any performance-enhancing drug, there's no way in the world he'll be willing to do that,' the policeman said.

'Correct. By looking at his previous medical history, we can see what a normal blood count is for him. If you look at the first set of results Jordanne looked at on Friday, you can see they're exactly the same as the test he had done four months ago.'

'Is that rare?'

'It's rare for *all* of the numbers to be exactly the same. His red and white blood cell count is exactly the same as the previous test,' Jordanne said.

'Indicating that the results have been falsified.' Dorne nodded, finally catching on. 'So where is this Ethan Hoe now?'

'Probably training at the IAS.'

'I might go and have a word with him.'

'Would you mind postponing it until Monday?' Alex asked.

'Why?' The policeman narrowed his gaze.

'As soon as word gets out that we're onto them, there's no telling what might happen. The hospital, the IAS and the athletes federation will all be involved. This is high media stuff.'

'Not to mention Dr McElroy here loses her job.'

'It's inevitable that I'll be losing my job,' Jordanne said, not looking at Alex. 'This needs to be brought out into the open, but by waiting until Monday it might force the hand of whoever is behind this fiasco. They've obviously been looking for the test results—the *real* ones—that weren't supposed to be sent to me. As they haven't found them, perhaps they think they're still in the mail system.'

'And they were where?'

'In Alex's car in the glovebox,' she said with a smile. 'It was unintentional. I just took them out on Friday night to show him later. As we were involved with an emergency and then returned to my house...' Jordanne trailed off and shrugged. 'We just didn't get around to looking at them until this afternoon.'

'I'll contact you on Monday morning and I don't want either of you doing anything heroic. Understand?'

They both nodded, feeling like schoolchildren. When the sergeant left, Jordanne relaxed into a chair with relief.

'How did your office look at the IAS?' Alex asked as he came to stand beside her.

'Like my apartment,' she answered.

'I want you to spend the rest of the weekend with me. I don't want you to be on your own.' He placed his hands on her shoulders and began to massage. 'Perhaps we can call Kirsten and ask her to come and help us clean up your apartment.'

Jordanne closed her eyes, relaxing even more beneath the masterful strokes of his hands. 'Hmm. I don't want to think about cleaning up *just* yet.'

His hands stilled on her shoulders and she turned to look up at him. 'What's wrong?'

He came around in front of her and leaned against his desk. 'We need to—'

'Talk,' she finished for him. 'Alex, if you're going to tell me about your marriage and divorce, right at this moment in time I don't want to know. It was in the *past*. Why can't we just leave it there?'

'Because in some instances the past affects the future. Actually, that wasn't what I was going to talk to you about but it is something we still need to discuss, Jordanne.'

'OK, but just not now.'

'All right. While you were at the IAS with Dorne, I searched the internet to find out who the parent company is of the pharmaceutical firm.' His tone held a note of worry in it and Jordanne's apprehension grew.

'And what did you find?' she asked, not sure she was going to like the answer.

He stared at her for a long moment before saying, 'It's The Bransford Corporation.'

Jordanne gasped. 'Norman Bransford's company? Sally's father?'

Alex nodded. 'Took me by surprise, too.'

'No.' Jordanne shook her head. 'There must be some mistake.'

'No mistake.'

'Is that why you wanted the police to wait until Monday before furthering their investigations?'

Alex nodded. 'I wanted to talk to Sally first. See what she could find out.'

'But her dad's recovering from his car accident. I remember it clearly—he was the first patient I operated on with you, here at Canberra General. From what Sally's said, he's not even back at work yet.'

'I know.'

'I guess in the past I wouldn't have been surprised if he'd been involved in something like this. My memories of Norman Bransford whilst I was at medical school aren't the most pleasant. He tried to bribe me to convince Sally to give up medicine.'

'I know all about your history with the Bransfords. Why do you think Jed was so against Sally when she first came to work with him? Anyway, that's water under the bridge now, because Norman Bransford *has* changed. Sally's own happiness is evidence of that.'

'So we talk to Sally and Jed when they get back tomorrow evening?'

'Yes. Perhaps Sally can talk to Norman who can get the internal wheels moving before the police crack this thing wide open. I don't want the people responsible to have an opportunity to cover things up. I want their fingers caught *in* the cookie jar.'

'You may need to get the police to postpone things for a bit longer than just Monday.'

'I realise that, but hopefully by then we would have received some word from Norman. The police can then work with him to ensure that everyone involved is caught and charged.'

'Why did Jed and Sally pick *this* weekend to go away?' Jordanne asked rhetorically.

Alex urged her to stand up before he pulled her onto his lap, wrapping his arms about her securely. 'As we're now *forced* to wait until their return,' he said as he nibbled at her ear lobe.

Jordanne shivered, her thoughts turning away from the research study. 'Hmm?' She closed her eyes and tipped her head back as he feathered light kisses down her neck.

'I suggest we put the time to good use,' Alex murmured.

'What do you have in mind?' she whispered. Alex placed a quick kiss on her lips and stood her on her feet. Jordanne's eyes snapped open in astonishment.

'That we get your apartment cleaned up.' With that, he

stood and crossed to his desk, picking up the phone. 'What's Kirsten's number?'

Amazingly enough, Jordanne almost enjoyed herself as the three of them cleaned up her apartment. Kirsten and Alex kept up a steady stream of jokes, turning what was supposed to be a tedious and unwelcome task into one that wasn't too bad.

The three of them went out to dinner before Alex and Jordanne said goodnight to Kirsten and returned to his home. As the previous night, Alex made her another milk drink but this time she was awake when he climbed into bed beside her. He gave her a quick kiss on the lips before gathering her into his arms.

'You have enough turmoil in your life at the moment,' he whispered as she dozed off. As her mind wound down and started slipping into dreamland, Jordanne wondered whether Alex was still afraid of emotionally hurting her. It was the main reason why she hadn't yet told him that she loved him. She was so conscious of taking it slowly with him, of not rushing him, but she wasn't a patient woman and she wouldn't wait for ever.

In the morning, Alex cooked Jordanne a hearty breakfast before they went shopping in the markets. She wondered whether part of his plan was to keep her out in crowds as they didn't return to his apartment until just before seven o'clock that evening.

She'd called her brother earlier that morning and asked if both he and Sally wouldn't mind coming to Alex's place on their way back from the airport. Jed's interest had been piqued.

Alex ordered Chinese take-away, which was delivered just as Jed's white Jaguar XJ6 pulled into the driveway.

'Have you two been working hard again?' Jed asked, and

all Jordanne could do was nod. It wasn't a lie—they *had* been working hard. As they sat down to dinner, Alex and Jordanne listened intently to Sally rave about the good time they'd had.

'Catching up with my parents and the rest of your brood,' she said, indicating Jordanne, 'was great fun. Thank you again, Alex, for that present. It was just what we needed. A weekend away.'

'I'm happy for you,' Alex replied.

'How…is your dad?' Jordanne asked, concerned that the news they had for Norman Bransford might not help his recovery.

'He's doing extremely well. I'm sure you've received an update from his orthopaedic surgeon in Sydney,' Sally said to Alex.

'Yes, but I guess what Jordanne is asking is how is he emotionally? Is he coping with staying at home? From what I remember of your father, he didn't like to be idle.'

Sally laughed. 'No, he doesn't, but he's doing a bit of work from home and that seems to satisfy him.'

'So why did you want to see us? Was it just to catch up on family matters?' Jed asked before his mouth closed over his chopsticks that were laden with food. He glanced from Jordanne to Alex and then back again.

'No. Well, yes, and, uh…no,' Jordanne fumbled. 'It's good to hear you had a great time,' she said, trying again. Her gaze rested on Sally and she took a deep breath. 'We need to tell you something that's been happening at work. More specifically, with the research study.'

She had their interest now. They both told the story of what had been happening and Alex showed them the X-rays and blood-test results which had been locked in his safe. 'The thing is,' Jordanne said, hoping that Sally wouldn't take things the wrong way, 'that when we checked into the parent of the pharmaceutical company, it was…the Bransford Corporation.'

'*What?*' Sally stared at Jordanne, completely amazed.

'That's why we wanted to talk to you,' Alex added. 'Perhaps you can talk to your father and see if he can dig internally before the police get completely involved because when that happens—'

'The media's involved as well,' Jed finished.

'I'll call Dad right now,' Sally said, and reached for her mobile phone. None of them pretended *not* to listen to her conversation and when she finally ended the call she smiled enthusiastically. 'He'll look into it right away and hopefully will have some answers by tomorrow evening. He suggested we ask the police to contact him tomorrow morning and he can take it from there.'

'Good,' Jordanne said, heaving a heavy sigh.

'Who'd like some dessert?' Alex asked. 'Triple chocolate ice cream,' he said temptingly.

'Why don't you just bring out the tub and four spoons?' Jordanne suggested with a smile at him. When he'd told her that he loved chocolate, she'd thought he'd been exaggerating. Now she realised he hadn't been.

As they all sat around, eating ice cream, Jordanne could tell that Sally was very worried about the situation.

'If you'll excuse us,' she said after Alex and Jed had polished off the rest of the ice cream, 'I'd like to get home and call my father again.'

'Of course,' Jordanne said. 'We appreciate any help both you and your father can give us.' She hugged her friend tightly before kissing her brother.

After they'd left, Jordanne slumped down onto the lounge and played with her hair, winding it around her finger.

'You're preoccupied about something,' Alex observed as

he came to sit beside her. 'I've noticed you always do that to your hair if you're preoccupied.'

Jordanne smiled at him. 'Why do you think I tie it back for work?'

Alex didn't smile but took her hand in his. 'It's time,' he said solemnly. 'We've avoided discussing my past for too long, Jordanne. It's time.'

# CHAPTER TEN

A BAND of apprehension tightened around Jordanne's heart. She'd put it off yesterday and today but now the moment of truth was here. She reached out and touched Alex's cheek, desperately trying to be strong for him. What he had to say was important, even if she didn't think it would impact upon their future together. The fact that it was important to him should make it important to her. Communication, she remembered her mother saying. Any good relationship was all about communication.

'I'm listening,' she said, and he turned his face and kissed her hand before placing it back in her lap.

'When I was twenty, still in med school, I got married.' His tone was neutral and Jordanne tried hard to read his expression but found she couldn't. 'We were young and impetuous but if there was one thing neither set of parents wanted it was an accidental pregnancy.' He laughed without humour. 'We should have been so lucky,' he mumbled, his tone laced with irony.

Jordanne remained silent, holding his hands with hers.

'My wife decided she wanted children straight away so we began trying.' He exhaled slowly, his gaze never leaving hers. 'Five years later, after every fertility test, drug or natural remedy under the sun, I signed the divorce papers. We had been unable to have children and it had wrecked our marriage.'

The band that clutched at Jordanne's heart tightened imperceptibly.

'It tore us both apart.' He was silent for a whole two

minutes and Jordanne wasn't sure whether she was supposed to say something or not. She searched her mind for words of sympathy but couldn't find any. All she could focus on were the words he'd said—'unable to have children'.

'Because of this...*information*, I've steered clear of any heavy emotional relationships for the past seventeen years. The scars are still there and, as you can see, it still hurts to discuss it.'

Tears welled in Jordanne's eyes as she empathised with the pain he was sharing.

'You, on the other hand, are different from any of those other relationships. I've fought my feelings for you with everything I had, but it wasn't enough.' He took a deep breath before confessing, 'You've become very special to me, Jordanne.'

Jordanne sighed and leaned forward to kiss him briefly on the lips, a watery smile on her lips.

Alex set her back and squeezed her hands. 'My feelings have grown, especially this last weekend. Just having you sharing my home, sleeping in my bed—it's made me realise that I don't want to wake up in the mornings unless you're there beside me.'

The tears spilled over onto Jordanne's cheeks and Alex tenderly wiped them away. 'Which is why I wanted to talk to you. It wouldn't have been fair to take our relationship to the next level without confessing my past. I know you want children, Jordanne. It's evident in *everything* about you. Your caring, nurturing qualities shine through so naturally, I can't imagine you living a life without children surrounding you.'

Jordanne's eyes widened in alarm and her breathing became shallow. 'What...what are you saying?'

Alex closed his eyes and groaned in frustration before

raking his hand through his hair. 'This is so hard for me to do.' He opened his eyes and looked at Jordanne, his jaw firmly set. 'We can't continue to see each other.'

'But I love you,' she said, and put her hand out to him.

Alex stood and started pacing the room. 'No,' he ground out fiercely. 'Don't love me. If you do, you'll be doomed to a childless marriage. Believe me—' the bitterness in his tone hit her with force '—I've been there. It's not something I'd recommend *anyone* to go through.'

Jordanne stood and took a few steps towards him but he held up his hands and she stopped. 'Alex, seventeen years is a long time,' she reasoned. 'There have been incredible breakthroughs in medical technology. Childless couples all around the world are having their dreams come true because of these new procedures.' She hesitated a moment before asking, 'Was there something medically wrong with your wife as well as yourself?'

'Yes.'

'See?' she said, clinging to the hope that was surging through her body. 'It might not be the case with me. *We* might stand a better chance. We can both have tests and then figure out what to do next.'

'Tests.' He spat the word. 'They're a joke. One test after another. Pinning your hopes on results and tearing away another piece of your soul when they come back negative. I've lived through this, Jordanne, and I care far too much about you to have you go through it.'

'That's my decision,' she said forcefully, placing one hand over her heart.

'Jordanne, it would tear us apart. I've been there, *remember*. I've *lived* that life and, quite frankly, I don't want to live it again.'

'We can adopt,' Jordanne suggested, desperately searching for an alternative.

He closed his eyes momentarily and shook his head before looking at her. 'Think about it, Jordanne. Adoption is nowhere near as easy now as it was in the past. My mother knows of a couple who have been on the adoption waiting list for almost six years now, with *still* no hope in sight.'

'At least they're trying,' Jordanne said, feeling her anger at his negative attitude spring forth. More tears rushed down her cheeks and she impatiently brushed them away. 'You're not even willing to give us a chance, Alex. You may have experienced what it was like to live through a childless marriage with another woman almost twenty years ago, but that doesn't mean the same thing would happen to *us*.'

'It…won't…work,' he said slowly. 'It's been seventeen years and I *still* feel the pain of it. *Every day.* I push it out of my mind, I do my best not to think about it and then there's Scott, about to have his *third* child. Do you have any idea how inadequate that makes me feel?' He was yelling now.

'That's the crux of the matter, isn't it?' Jordanne said carefully, and stared at him in astonishment. 'The fact that you don't think you're *man* enough to produce an heir. You're not even willing to look at the possibility that a lot of people survive quite happily in childless marriages, whether it was intentional or not.'

'*How dare you?*'

'How dare *you*? Lumping me in with other statistics. Not even *willing* to give our relationship the chance it deserves.'

'You're lucky I gave it *this* much of a chance.'

'What's that supposed to mean?'

'I wanted to break it off as soon as it began because I *knew* I'd hurt you.' His words plunged the room back into silence—an empty silence that held no hope.

'Well, you were right,' she said eventually, her voice

breaking on the words. 'You *did* hurt me.' Jordanne sniffed and wiped again at the tears that refused to be stopped. 'You had already decided before you told me that there was no future for us. You're not even willing to compromise.' She took a ragged breath in. 'You're just giving up because it's *too* hard.'

Jordanne stormed from the room and began shoving her clothes into her bag, her vision blurred from the tears that continued to fall. She retrieved her toiletries from the bathroom before zipping the bag closed with finality. After locating her handbag, she walked back into the lounge room to find Alex still standing where she'd left him.

'I think we both need some time, Alex.'

'It's over, Jordanne,' he said flatly, before walking from the room.

His words incensed her once more and Jordanne reached for her mobile phone as she let herself out of his house. She called a taxi and waited in the cold night for it to arrive. At least it wasn't raining, she reasoned, trying desperately to look for the silver lining in this very dark cloud.

As she let herself into her dark and cold apartment, Jordanne walked through to her bedroom, not switching on any lights. Dumping her bags at the foot of the bed, she threw herself down onto the pillows and allowed the tears that she'd held back so valiantly in the taxi to spill out.

She cried herself to sleep and woke at around three o'clock, feeling cold. She huddled beneath the covers, her misery once more bringing tears to her eyes. Two wonderful nights of having Alex's arms around her and now here she was, alone and cold. She yearned for him—body, mind and soul—but at the moment the situation looked hopeless.

She reached for the spare pillow beside her and cuddled into it. 'Alex,' she whispered into the dark, her tone filled with despair. 'I need you.' The sobs came once more, tearing at her soul before they eventually subsided into small hiccups.

Taking a deep breath, Jordanne finally drifted off to sleep once more and was awoken by the buzzing of her alarm clock. Feeling as though her entire body was made of lead, she went through the motions of getting ready for work when all she really felt like doing was going back to bed and feeling sorry for herself.

During ward round and clinic, she and Alex ignored each other completely, their gazes rarely meeting. If they needed to speak, they used monosyllables. Jordanne wondered how many staff members picked up on their attitudes but then decided that she didn't really care. The hospital grapevine could buzz all it wanted. Thanks to the doping at the IAS, she'd soon be out of a job and that meant out of this hospital—away from Alex.

Even as she thought about it, Jordanne felt fresh tears prick behind her eyes. After clinic, she decided the best thing to do was to get out of the hospital. Returning to her office, she grabbed her bag, locked her office and quickly walked out of the department and over to the doctors' car park.

Her mobile phone rang as she climbed behind the wheel. She looked at the number of the caller which was registered on her phone's screen. It was Alex's secretary's number. Jordanne put the phone down, letting the call go through to her message bank.

She ignored it until she'd pulled into the car park at the private hospital where Roberto Portatello was recovering after his total hip replacement. Listening to the message, Alex's secretary merely told her of an appointment they had later that afternoon with the police to discuss the research project.

She pushed the thoughts from her mind and took a deep

breath. She was a professional who was about to see a patient. There was no room for personal problems here.

'You've had a lovers' tiff,' Roberto announced only moments after she'd walked into his room. Jordanne looked up at him, amazed. 'I told you I was good at reading people. Do you want to talk about it?'

'No, thanks.'

'You'll sort it out,' he told her. 'You and Dr Page were meant to be together.'

Jordanne looked down at Roberto's chart and clenched her teeth to control her emotions. Taking a deep breath, she smiled up at him. 'How are you feeling?'

'As well as can be expected.'

She gave him a check-up. 'Everything seems fine,' she reported.

'Good. Now, tell me what you found out with your research project.' Roberto's eyes sparkled with anticipatory delight.

Jordanne laughed and it felt good. Roberto nodded thoughtfully as she told him everything that had transpired in the past forty-eight hours concerning the pharmaceutical company.

'That must have scared the life out of you, coming home to find your place in such a mess,' he tut-tutted. 'But desperate people do desperate things.'

'That they do,' Jordanne replied with a sigh. She wondered just how desperate Alex was to push her away. He'd said that he didn't want to hurt her but couldn't he see that he was hurting *both* of them by not giving their relationship a chance?

'And you say the blood-test results were with you the entire time? Imagine their fury after turning both of your offices inside out and then your apartment and car and *still* not finding what they were looking for.' This made Roberto laugh, a deep, rich rumbling sound that was contagious. Jordanne joined in. Yes, visiting her patient had been the tonic she'd required to help reorganise her thoughts.

'I can see the looks on their faces. Where are those reports? Where has she hidden them? Is she onto us?' He laughed again. 'You would have had them in a right tizz. Good girl, I'm proud of you.'

'I didn't do it on purpose. At that stage I had no idea what was going on. I was just heartily confused.'

This made Roberto laugh even more. 'Even better.' Slowly he calmed down. 'I love it when the bad guys get what they deserve.' He reached out a hand to Jordanne. When she took it he said, 'Thank you. Thank you for coming and sharing this with an old man and bringing a touch of colour back into my life.' He raised her hand to his lips and kissed it briefly.

Jordanne felt herself begin to blush as he released her hand. 'Let me check your wound site again. I hope you haven't popped any sutures with all that laughing.'

'Even if I have, it would have been worth it.'

Jordanne checked the site but amazingly everything was fine. She stayed a few minutes more before heading back to the hospital for the debrief. As she parked her car in the doctors' car park, she saw Sally's Mercedes parked across the way and realised that she, and probably Jed, were here for the debriefing as well.

'You're a few minutes late,' Alex's secretary told her as Jordanne rushed up the corridor.

'I know. Sorry.'

'They haven't started. I've just taken the teas and coffees in and there's one there for you.'

'Thanks,' Jordanne said as she pushed open the departmental conference-room door, apologising for being late. There was only one seat left and that was next to Alex. It would have looked churlish as well as suspicious if she asked everyone to shift around so that she didn't have to sit next to him.

Senior Sergeant Dorne, who was in charge of the investigation, began the discussion by giving a brief background on the events so far. As the meeting progressed, Jordanne kept her gaze away from Alex and concentrated hard on what was being said, which was difficult, given that she couldn't help but smell the scent of his cologne, which she'd become very accustomed to in the past few weeks.

When his leg accidentally touched hers beneath the table, Jordanne gasped in surprise, a spiral of desire coursing throughout her entire body. Dorne stopped speaking and everyone looked at her. She smiled, completely embarrassed, and cleared her throat.

'You were saying?' she prompted, and the debrief continued.

Jordanne glanced across at Sally, who was trying not to smile, and Jordanne lowered her head, her embarrassment increasing.

Taking a slow and steady breath, Jordanne moved her legs as far away from Alex's as possible and forced her attention back to the topic at hand.

'What's the report from the Bransford Corporation?' Alex asked Sally.

'Senior Sergeant Dorne and I flew to Sydney this morning where we had a meeting with the investigators. Dad has had people working on it since I spoke to him last night. From what they've discovered so far, it's one of the smaller research and development departments of the pharmaceutical company which was responsible for falsifying the data.'

'The medication you're using in your study is a…' Dorne

looked down at his notes '…non-performance-enhancing drug. Correct?'

'Correct,' Alex replied.

'This company discovered that when the medication was given to people who *hadn't* sustained fractures, it *became* a performance-enhancing drug,' Dorne announced.

'That means that none of those athletes the company recommended have ever had fractures.' Jordanne nodded, the pieces finally falling into place. 'That was why they had to falsify the X-rays and the test results.'

'Exactly. Mr Bransford has agreed to give the investigation his full support and co-operation so hopefully some time this week we'll be pressing formal charges against those persons involved. I'll make sure you receive a copy of the full report.'

'If the athletes were being doped, then the coach would have been in on it, too.' Jordanne nodded. 'That would explain his attitude towards me.'

'Just from the preliminary investigations,' Sally said, 'it appears they had an operative at the X-ray place and at the path labs. People who could easily get their hands on the data and change the names and dates.'

Alex shook his head. 'The lengths they've gone to. What about Jordanne's job?' Alex was the one to pose the question and she wondered whether he was as eager to have her gone as she was to leave.

'My father would like to assure you both that Jordanne's position as research fellow will remain until the end of the contract as stipulated in the original agreement,' Sally said proudly. 'You can continue with your research into bone regeneration.'

Jordanne was shocked. She looked at Sally.

'Aren't you happy?' Jed asked.

'Uh…of course.' Jordanne quickly recovered and remembered her manners. 'Please, thank your father for me,' she said to Sally.

'When he learned that the research project concerned you and Alex, he was determined to make sure you kept your job. After all, you were the ones who had operated on him after his car accident.'

'But it's our job.'

'Well, he sees it as part of his job to ensure the contracts his companies undertake are adhered to.'

'All right,' Jordanne said, nodding. Now she had to spend the rest of this year working with Alex. How was she going to cope?

There wasn't that much more to discuss and when the debriefing was over it was almost time to leave for the day.

Jordanne said goodbye to Sally and Jed before hurrying to her office. She tidied up her desk and locked her drawers. When the knock came on her door, she braced herself.

Jed entered without a word and closed the door behind him.

'Feel like talking?' he asked as he crossed to her side. Protectively, Jed placed his arms around her and Jordanne relaxed against him.

'You know, don't you?' she whispered, and leaned back to look up at her brother.

'If you're referring to Alex being unable to have children, yes. He told me on Monday.'

Jordanne broke free from his grasp. 'He's not even willing to give us a chance, Jed. I can understand his pain and I feel for him, I *really* do but he just shut me out. He says he won't go through tests again. That he doesn't want to have another childless relationship.' Jordanne bit her lower lip to stop it from wobbling.

'I love him, Jed. Almost from the first instant I saw him, I've loved him.' Jordanne's despair was evident in her tone.

'I don't know what we're going to do. I don't see how we can continue to work together for the rest of this year.'

'Ah, Jordanne,' he sighed, and gathered her into his arms again. 'Do you want me to talk to him?'

'No. I know you mean well and I know he's your friend but if Alex loves me, *really* loves me, then he wouldn't be doing this to us. He'd be accepting whatever we could have together.'

'I don't know what to tell you, kiddo.'

Jordanne leaned up and kissed his cheek. 'Just being here is enough, Jed. You're a good brother. Thanks.'


'And what about that hit-and-run patient you had?' Sally asked just after the waiter had refreshed their drinks. She was wearing a lovely navy blue dress made out of raw Thai silk but Sally was the type of person who could wear a garbage bag and still look incredible.

'Louise Kellerman?'

'That's the one,' Sally replied. 'How's she coping?'

Jordanne knew what Sally was up to. She was trying to keep her friend's mind off the fact that Alex hadn't turned up at her parents' wedding anniversary party. It had been going now for a good two hours, yet still there was no sign of him. 'Louise is doing well. The police have caught and charged the person responsible for the hit and run. It means Louise will have to testify in court eventually but she now has some very good support on her side.'

'What do you mean?'

'She's in love with the ward social worker.'

'Dean?' Sally's eyes widened in disbelief. 'How does he feel about that?'

'The same as Louise.'

'I hope he's transferred her care,' Sally said.

'Yes, he has. She has a few more weeks in traction because of the pelvic fracture, before being transferred to the rehabilitation hospital, but she's progressing very well.'

'Good for them,' Sally said heartily.

Jordanne looked down into her drink. 'Yeah, good for them,' she said without feeling. She looked up at Sally and gave her a watery smile. 'When is it going to be good for me?'

Sally put her drink down and placed her arm around Jordanne's shoulders. 'Everything will work out fine. Trust me.'

'Do you know something?' Jordanne asked curiously.

'No,' Sally answered honestly. 'I just know that Alex does love you, Jordanne, but he's just having a hard time coming to terms with what it means.'

Kirsten came over to them and put her arm around Jordanne as well. She was wearing a pair of black trousers and a stunning beaded jacket. With her auburn locks falling softly to the middle of her back, Jordanne knew that her friend had turned a few heads as she'd walked across the room.

'Is this a secret meeting or can anyone join in?'

Jordanne laughed. 'Only you and no one else,' she warned.

'Hey, how's that gunman you operated on?'

'He's doing fine. Did you two get together and decide what topics would be best to keep my mind off the fact that Alex isn't coming?' Jordanne looked from one friend to the other. They both looked extremely guilty and nodded, confirming her suspicions.

'Well, thank you,' Jordanne said, not about to begrudge them. 'You're both fantastic friends but can't we talk about something other than patients? This is supposed to be a party, not a departmental meeting.'

Sally and Kirsten laughed. 'What would you like to talk about?' Sally asked.

'How about Joel?'

'What about Joel?' Kirsten asked as all three of them looked across the room to where Jordanne's brother was in deep discussion with Jed.

'It's eight weeks since he had surgery to his knee, and from what he mentioned to me the other day on the phone he's looking for part-time work as a locum GP.' Jordanne looked expectantly at Kirsten. 'Any chance you have some extra work you need help with at your practice?'

'That's right,' Sally chimed in. 'You said to me only the other day that you were thinking about employing a locum.'

Kirsten ummed and ahhed for a moment before saying, 'The practice is at the stage where I either need to expand or contract.'

'A bit uncertain about things?' Jordanne asked.

'Yes and no,' Kirsten replied. 'I'm still thinking things through. Don't get me wrong, I love being a GP but…I don't know. Things just don't feel…right.'

'I'm sure you'll work it out, but from a personal angle I'd love to have Joel move to Canberra.'

Sally laughed. 'Three McElroys in one very small state.'

'Territory,' Kirsten corrected. 'The Australian Capital *Territory*.'

'I stand corrected,' Sally said with a smile. 'But regardless of what it's called, I'm not sure the good people of Canberra would be able to cope.'

'It's an invasion,' Kirsten joined in as they laughed.

For the first time that evening, Jordanne grasped at the happiness she felt in her heart. So what if Alex wasn't here! So what if he didn't want to work things out! So what if he didn't love her.

The last thought brought the melancholy back with a

vengeance. Her heart ached for him, her mind begged for the stimulating conversations they used to enjoy. Her soul was suffocating without him and her body longed to be held once more in his arms, his lips pressed firmly against her own—where they belonged.

'Excuse me,' Jed said as he walked towards them. 'I've come to break up your tête-à-tête.'

'I suppose you've shared your fiancée enough for one night, eh?' Jordanne asked him.

'That's not why I came over,' he said, although he took the opportunity to give Sally a kiss. 'Actually, little sister, I've come to ask you to dance.'

'Oh.' Jordanne was surprised for a moment. 'OK.' She smiled at her friends as Jed whisked her out onto the dance floor.

'How are you holding up?' he asked, concerned.

Jordanne sighed. 'I'm getting there.'

'You have bags under your eyes and Mum is very worried. Why don't you have a talk to her?'

'Maybe you're right. I could do with some of Mum's wisdom right about now.'

Jed continued to dance her around the room. 'I played squash yesterday afternoon with Alex,' he said.

Jordanne's heart rate increased and she gave her brother a wary look. 'What did you say?'

'Not at lot. He was in a rotten mood but he won every game.'

'I don't suppose he asked about me?'

'No, but I ventured the information that you weren't very happy and he only continued to smash that little black ball even harder. So, what are *you* going to do?'

'I honestly don't know. I told him that I'd be willing to have tests, that we could look at adoption—*anything*. Jed, we belong together. I can compromise. I can live a life without children.' Even as she said the words, Jordanne felt a deep ache begin in her heart.

'Can you? You don't sound too sure, Jordanne.'

'My alternative is life without Alex and I definitely know I won't survive that.' She wiped carefully at the tears before they spilt over her lashes, ruining her make-up. 'I think I've had enough dancing, Jed.' As soon as the words were out of her mouth, Jordanne felt a finger tap her shoulder and she turned around, only to gaze into Alex's blue eyes. Her breathing increased and her knees started to give way but thankfully Jed's strong arms came around her.

Alex was here! He was here! Her heart sang with elation as she glanced at him. He was wearing a pair of denim jeans and tatty old running shoes. An open-necked shirt and a sports jacket almost testified to him having left home in somewhat of a hurry.

'Here,' Jed said as he all but dumped Jordanne onto Alex. 'I think she belongs to you.'

Alex had no option but to hold Jordanne in his arms and at the simple touch of his body against hers Jordanne stiffened, the signals finally getting through to her knees. She stood and glared at him for another moment.

She was aware that a few people around them had started watching, taking in Alex's appearance with amused smiles. As all the other males in the room were dressed in tuxedos, he did look a little out of place.

'You look…breathtaking,' he whispered, his gaze travelling the length of her long white satin gown. It had diamanté straps and a long split in the skirt that went from her ankle almost to the top of her thigh. Her hair was loose, its dark, rich colour beautifully complementing the dress.

He didn't look so bad either. In fact, Jordanne had never thought him more handsome than he was at this particular point in time.

'So you decided to come after all,' she said, amazed at how calm her voice sounded because she felt far from calm.

'Jordanne, we need to talk.'

'Huh. The last time you said that, you broke my heart.' Anger prevailed. Jordanne spun on her heel and started walking from the dancing area. Alex reached for her hand. 'Wait, Jordanne,' he said, but she snatched her hand free. 'Jordanne?'

She knew she was being stubborn but she didn't want to talk. Not again. She wanted *action*.

'Will you just *stop*!' he yelled impatiently, and everyone around them did as he suggested. Even the band stopped playing. The entire room was plunged into silence and Jordanne looked slightly startled.

Alex, however, seemed oblivious to everyone in the room except her. 'Jordanne,' he said with a hint of warning in his tone. 'We *need* to talk.'

'Why?' she answered carefully, her gaze captured by his.

'Because I've made a mistake.'

Her heart breathed a small sigh of relief but she remained outwardly unmoved. 'Yes.'

'I'm going insane without you. I need you, Jordanne.'

'Why?' she whispered, tears blurring her eyes, her breath caught in her throat. It seemed as though the rest of the room held their breath as well, waiting for Alex to say the words that Jordanne so desperately needed to hear. 'Why, Alex?' she urged when he was silent for a long moment.

'Because I love you and I need you beside me for the rest of my life.'

Jordanne closed her eyes, unable to keep the tears from spilling over. The next thing she felt was Alex's hands cradling her face before his lips were pressed against her own. 'I love you,' he said again between kisses.

Jordanne opened her eyes and looked up at him through

her tears. Tenderly he kissed them away. 'I love you, Jordanne.'

The room was still in a stunned silence as Alex took Jordanne's hand in his and got down on bended knee. 'My life is meaningless without you, Jordanne. Please, come and fill it with the sunshine that radiates from deep within you. Marry me?'

Jordanne brushed the tears away from her face, not caring about ruining her make-up. Her head felt light and was spinning with complete happiness. Alex had come. Alex did love her. Alex wanted to marry her. The fact that he was here, on bended knee—surely that meant he was willing to have tests, to pursue the dream of a family with her?

She glanced down at him and felt the room begin to lurch and spin. She looked up quickly at the smiling faces all around her—her parents, who were holding hands, her siblings and her friends.

The room spun again and as Jordanne looked down at Alex the tension and emotional roller-coaster she'd been riding for the past seven days appeared to catch up with her. She closed her eyes and raised her hand to her temple before she pitched forwards, her mind going blank. The last thing she recalled was Alex's strong arms around her.

'She'll be fine,' she heard her mother's voice saying as someone applied a cool cloth to her forehead.

'I never faint,' she mumbled, and received a rich laugh in reply.

'Well, honey, you just did.'

Jordanne opened her eyes in a dimly lit room—her parents' bedroom. It made sense. All the other bedrooms were upstairs.

'I'll leave you two alone,' Jane McElroy said and made a discreet exit.

'How are you feeling?' Alex asked with concern.

'Tired,' Jordanne answered with a small smile. 'You're here,' she said, reaching out to touch his cheek.

'Yes. I'm here.'

'I didn't think you were coming.'

'Neither did I, hence the way I'm dressed. Yesterday when Jed said you were miserable, the knowledge started gnawing at me because I knew *I'd* been the one to make you miserable. I wasn't planning on attending, but as I prowled around my house for the umpteenth time all I could think about was you. The way you made us coffee, helped me with the dishes, showered in my bathroom and slept in my bed.' His gaze darkened as he said the last and Jordanne shivered with excitement.

'Everywhere I looked there were reminders of you and I couldn't stand it any more. I realised that children or no children—I *need you*. I called the airport, managed to get the last seat on a flight to Sydney and then it took almost longer than the flight to get from the airport to your house. I think the taxi driver thought I was a lunatic until I told him I was on my way to propose to the most beautiful woman in the world.

'When I arrived at your parents' door, I realised I probably should have changed my clothes before I came, but I just wasn't thinking straight.'

Jordanne was happy that he was here but they still had issues to resolve. 'What about children, Alex? What are we going to do?'

'We'll go through the tests. You were right about medical technology. The chances of childless couples conceiving are now quite high. I want to take that chance, Jordanne, and I want to take it with you.'

'And if we *can't* have children?'

'It doesn't matter, Jordanne. I *need* you. I've changed a lot since I was twenty-five, and although the ache of not being able to have a family is for ever present in my life, not being able to have you by my side for the rest of my life isn't worth even contemplating. How about you? How would you feel if we can't conceive?'

'I honestly don't know, Alex, but I do know one thing. With you by my side, I feel as though I can conquer anything. We draw strength from each other, we give to each other and the past week of thinking about a life without you has almost destroyed me.'

'I know,' he said. 'And I'm sorry.'

'Shh,' she said, and placed a finger over his lips. 'Kiss me, Alex.'

'With pleasure,' he replied, and bent over the bed to press his lips to hers. 'I love you, Jordanne. Without you, I'm only half a person. Make me whole. Make *us* whole. Marry me.'

'Yes,' she whispered as she levered herself up and straightened the straps on her dress. Alex plunged his fingers into her hair before burying his face in her neck. 'Yes, my love.'

'I don't think I'll ever get over how incredible you feel or smell or taste.' His breath fanned her neck. Jordanne giggled, feeling goose-bumps encompass her body in a tidal wave.

'This is how it will always be,' she prophesied. 'We'll always be in love.'

'That we will.' Alex helped her to her feet. 'Are you sure you're feeling all right?'

'I'm fine.' Jordanne smoothed the white satin down over her midriff.

'You're incredibly sexy,' Alex growled before he claimed her lips once more. 'Even more so in *that* dress. After we're married, I can see we're going to have trouble going out to dinner.'

'Why?'

'If you continue to wear these seductive outfits, we're never going to be leaving the bedroom.'

'Sounds good to me,' she whispered, and pressed her lips against his. 'You are so perfect for me, Alexander Page.'

'And you for me, Jordanne McElroy.'

'I think we have some explaining to do,' she said, gesturing to the door and the party beyond.

Alex tightened his hold on her and kissed her neck once more. 'I think…' he kissed his way up towards her mouth '…that they can wait…' his lips said against her, 'for a bit longer.'

**Modern Romance**™
...seduction and
passion guaranteed

**Tender Romance**™
...love affairs that
last a lifetime

**Sensual Romance**™
...sassy, sexy and
seductive

*Blaze*
...sultry days and
steamy nights

**Medical Romance**™
...medical drama on
the pulse

**Historical Romance**™
...rich, vivid and
passionate

*29 new titles every month.*

*With all kinds of Romance for
every kind of mood...*

MILLS & BOON®

*Makes any time special*™

MAT4

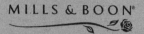

MILLS & BOON®

# Medical Romance™

### EMERGENCY WEDDING by *Marion Lennox*

When Dr Susie Ellis returns to the surgery she part-owns in Whale Beach, Australia, she finds the handsome Dr Darcy Hayden in residence. She needs to work to support her coming baby and he can't leave because of his young son, but only one doctor can stay at the small practice. Unless they get married…

### A NURSE'S PATIENCE by *Jessica Matthews*

Part 2 of Nurses Who Dare

Experience had taught Dr Ryan Gregory to be wary of his colleagues, and his outgoing nurse practitioner, Amy Wyman, was furious that he wanted to monitor her work. Her fiery nature was making him nervous professionally—and passionate in private. Unless Amy learnt some patience and Ryan started to trust, their lives were going to implode.

### ENGAGING DR DRISCOLL by *Barbara Hart*

Petra must resist her feelings for the gorgeous new doctor at her practice, as he is obviously involved with someone else, and Petra is engaged! Adam has other ideas, believing that Petra deserves someone better than her fiancé—like himself?

## On sale 2nd November 2001

# 4 FREE

### books and a surprise gift!

We would like to take this opportunity to thank you for reading this Mills & Boon® book by offering you the chance to take FOUR more specially selected titles from the Medical Romance™ series absolutely FREE! We're also making this offer to introduce you to the benefits of the Reader Service™—

- ★ FREE home delivery
- ★ FREE gifts and competitions
- ★ FREE monthly Newsletter
- ★ Exclusive Reader Service discounts
- ★ Books available before they're in the shops

Accepting these FREE books and gift places you under no obligation to buy, you may cancel at any time, even after receiving your free shipment. Simply complete your details below and return the entire page to the address below. *You don't even need a stamp!*

**YES!** Please send me 4 free Medical Romance books and a surprise gift. I understand that unless you hear from me, I will receive 6 superb new titles every month for just £2.49 each, postage and packing free. I am under no obligation to purchase any books and may cancel my subscription at any time. The free books and gift will be mine to keep in any case.

M1ZEA

Ms/Mrs/Miss/Mr ...........................Initials.....................................
BLOCK CAPITALS PLEASE
Surname ........................................................................................
Address ........................................................................................
...................................................................................................
..............................................................Postcode...............................

**Send this whole page to:**
**UK: FREEPOST CN81, Croydon, CR9 3WZ**
**EIRE: PO Box 4546, Kilcock, County Kildare (stamp required)**